Justice To All!

Gary M. Allen Sr.

ISBN 978-1-4958-0520-2
eISBN 978-1-4958-0521-9

Published July 2015

INFINITY PUBLISHING
1094 New DeHaven Street, Suite 100
West Conshohocken, PA 19428-2713
Toll-free (877) BUY BOOK
Local Phone (610) 941-9999
Fax (610) 941-9959
Info@buybooksontheweb.com
www.buybooksontheweb.com

ABOUT THIS NOVEL

This thrilling mystery is a story all readers can relate to. It's serious, funny, and sad.

It's about a young man Tim Ripple who's on a journey to find his family and his mother's killer. Tim had a different childhood as he went from one foster home to another. He tries to stay out of trouble, but trouble comes his way.

His life is about to change when he accidentally runs into a motorcycle club that helps him out in life.

As life goes on Tim is married had one child and is hit with an unexpected divorce.

Tim starts a new job not knowing his boss is affiliated with the mob. Tim works hard and puts himself through law school, he is about to take his bar examination when he is accused and picked up for murder.

About The Author

Mr. Gary Allen Sr. lived in Connecticut for many years where he taught part-time at a local community college.

Mr. Allen loves to travel, he has been in Asia and the Caribbean. Europe will be his next place of travel one of these days.

Mr. Allen also has published two other books Popular Drinks and Learn How To Bartend. He loves to write and teach and is working on another novel now.

He currently resides in South Florida with his wife and two playful cats.

Acknowledgements

I would like to thank my wonderful wife, Globee for all your help and encouragement.

I like to thank my son Gary Jr for all his great photos.

To my sister Constance thanks for all your help.

I like to thank Ray for all your help and kindness that you had share with me through my life. Ray is no longer with us but in spirit. He is looking down and laughing as he read this story.

And most of all I like to thank the man upstairs Dear Lord for all your great help and blessings in my life.

TABLE OF CONTENTS

CHAPTER ONE

LIFE IS NOT ALWAYS FAIR

Before you get too comfortable reading my story, grab a tall glass of ice water and something to munch on. It will be a while before you think about putting this book down, unless nature is calling you.! Ha! ha I'm only joking.

Also, I would like to say thank you for picking up my book. I hope you enjoy reading it as much as I enjoyed writing, and living it. I'm hoping that one of these days this novel well hit the movie theaters.

Hello, my name is Tim Ripple. Or so I was told from a few different foster parents that I had stayed with over the years. My life started in the state of Rhode Island on a beach, before I was brought to a small library, where my mother had left me at just two years old.

I was found in a stroller, wrapped in a blanket and covered with sand. Not to mention, a soiled diaper. Mom was gone and nowhere to be found. I was crying and screaming in the backroom in a corner where I was left with only a book in my stroller. Finally, a librarian discovered me and had sent one of her employees to the store to get some baby food and diapers. After she had changed and fed me, she played with me for a while. Then not too long after two men in blue took me away.

As life went on, I went from one foster home to another. I never knew who my biological mother and father were, and was always being tossed between families. I would get used to living with one family I really enjoyed being with, then all of a sudden the foster program Kids Youth Services, would just ship my ass to a different family. It was all so strange and very puzzling to me. But I had no say in any of it. When I'd lived with families I hated being with, it would take forever for the program to transfer me to another family.

Going from house to house was crap, and I was getting so tired and depressed. I kept on racking my brain, thinking there must be a better way to live. It is not normal for any kid to go through this punishment.

By the age of nine, I had lived with six different families in three different states. Nothing was consistent and most of the time, it felt like I would just be placed with whoever my social worker Mrs. Turner, knew and liked the most. I always believed that Mrs. Turner was getting a kickback from the families she had sent me to. There was no love, nothing but cold families with them. It was all about money they were getting for taking me in. It was so obvious in the way the families treated me, they didn't care or want a kid. They just wanted a paycheck. Enough brain racking, I will just get pissed and more confused.

It sure did feel like I was being punished most of the time, but I was glad about one thing. I had one person who later in my life became a close friend. His name was Duke Singer, and he was always there watching out for me. He really helped me cope with a lot that I couldn't understand in my life.

It was almost two years later, school had just ended. I was eleven years old and for once, looking forward to a summer with school friends. I had been staying with the Bell family in North Alabama and I liked it so far, though I hadn't been there long before I was told I was going to another new family in South Georgia, the Thompson.

I remember that dreadful day I met the Thompsons. It was as strange then, as it was the whole time I was there. Mrs. Thompson was soft spoken and gentle and I had a warm feeling about her. I wish she would have been around more, she always seemed so distant. Mr. Thompson hardly ever spoke, and when he did it was rough. He was always around watching me, sitting too close to me when the television was on.

There were times he'd come into my room when I'd be changing or he'd be there when I woke up. Once I locked the door and he told me I wasn't allowed to. When Mrs. Thompson wasn't around, and I'd be doing my homework at the kitchen table he'd come check up on me, rubbing my back and looking over my shoulder. This happened all the time and he wouldn't just leave me alone.

One late Saturday morning Mrs. Thompson went out shopping. It was just me and Mr. Thompson at home alone. Mr. Thompson had made a sexual pass at me. I ran fast into the kitchen to get away. He ran after me, he grabbed my waist and picked me up. I started to yell and scream and was kicking him hard, so he would let me go but he wouldn't. I didn't know what to do. He was pulling me through the kitchen and my hands reached for anything I could. I grabbed a knife from the counter as he was carrying me out of the kitchen, and without thinking I stabbed him in the leg three times and he finally let me go.

Mr. Thompson fell to the living floor yelling, and raising his fists, and I watched blood just start pouring out from his leg, all over the new tan living room rug that was just installed last week. What a freaking mess. I was in shock, and so pissed and confused that I left him there in the living room. I could not stand to see that pervert again.

I walked over to the dining room and turned the stereo on. I even raised the volume up to drown out the groans and yells of Mr. Thompson. I just didn't want to hear him anymore. Then I went into the kitchen to wash all the blood off of my arms and my hands, and then realized I was hungry, so I made myself a peanut butter and jelly sandwich and poured a large glass of chocolate milk. While I was chowing down, I was thinking, what I should do next. I listened for Mr. Thompson and no longer heard the groans, so I knew he had passed out.

As I was about to call the police, I heard a loud banging coming from the front door, so I went to answer it. Two policemen stood tall as I opened the door, they had said our next door neighbor, heard loud screaming coming from the house. Before I could say a word, they both noticed my bloody shirt. One of the cops pushed me to the ground and held me there, as he asked me where the blood was from. The other cop found Mr. Thompson in the other room, on his last leg almost — dead.

An ambulance was on its way to take him to the hospital. The police took me to the police station for questioning. I had told the cops my side of the story, and what Mr. Thompson was trying to do to me, but they put me in the jail for four days.

Before I knew it, I was sentenced to Longevity Reform School for two years. I would of have been there longer, but I think the Judge knew I told the truth. When the police found Mr. Thompson, he had only a pair of boxers on, I believed the Judge felt sorry for me.

I have so many questions that no one seemed to want to answer them. Why did mom leave me and never came back? What is up with that? Where is my so-called Dad? Do I have any blood brothers or sisters? Do I have any cousins, aunts, or uncles? If so, where the hell are they, why aren't they helping me?

A few foster parents whom I had lived with over the years, all had different stories about my family. Two different foster parents told me that I had two older brothers somewhere, but no sisters. And yet, no one seemed to know where they lived. I had been searching for both for many years with no luck. One family showed me a newspaper clipping about my Dad it stated he was a commercial fisherman in the State of Maine. The article read that on one cold, stormy, foggy night in December out in the sea, my Dad was working with a crew of 16 on board a big ship. They were trying to pull in all the fishing nets. The coastguard called the Captain to tell him the storm was heading their way. The Captain was told to head west, so they could avoid the worst part of the storm.

It was too late, the water was so rough and the waves were huge and they came over the vessel and swept up six men, who went overboard. The crew pulled one of the men out from the water. Dad was one of the five men that they couldn't save. The radio on the ship was destroyed from the storm. The captain could not call in for help or report what had happened.

Three days later, the ship arrived back to the port. Their captain reported the incident to the police and the coast guard. The local newspaper in town had an article about the five missing guys. The paper did mention that, Dad had lived and grow up in a small fishing town, in Sebastian, Florida. Then Dad moved to Bangor, Maine where he had died at 36, divorced and had three kids. Ours names, ages, or where any of kids lived, was never mentioned. There was no clue where to find my family. I went online and did research to find out about my Mom. The internet to my surprise had a few sad articles about Mom's death. One had read that my Mom was *murdered* three weeks after she had dropped me off at the library. The Mississippi police found her body with three nine millimeter bullet holes: two through her head, one bullet through the left side of her back. Moms right shoe was missing, along with her two chopped off toes, nowhere to be found. Two rings on the left hand were missing along with fresh needle tracks in her left upper arm. Her body was found lying in a big puddle of blood, in a parked car at a parking garage at the casino. When they did the autopsy and tests, heroin was found in her system. Mom was also raped and sexually abused and her panties were missing.

The article made me furious, the police never found the killer or killers! What I still find very baffling though, is that the article mentioned the police found Mom's pocketbook open in the backseat of her car with $10,000 in cash.

The killer never took the money. They did however, take Mom's toes instead. I do hope that Mom was already dead before they took her toes, so she did not have to feel the pain. With today's technology, they could find Moms killer in a heartbeat. I would like to know what they did with all the evidence they had collected. Also, why haven't the police found Moms killer? Now years later this is still a cold case. Mom was not rich, or famous. No one really cares to solve the case. We both know, that if Mom was one of those cop's mother, this investigation would have been solved at once, and I would not be having this conversation. One of these days I plan to investigate myself and find out who is responsible for my Mom's death.

When my time was up at the Reform School, Kids Youth Services had sent me to Detroit, where I would be staying with a new family, The Carters.

I still had a grudge against the world, and wasn't looking forward meeting them. From what I was told, they were in their early 60's, which would make them the oldest foster parents I've had so far. They never had any kids of their own, or foster kids for that matter, and I was their first prize.

Mrs. Carter was a peach. She was sweet, kind and caring, but the poor woman had a serious problem from what I noticed and that was her husband. Mr. Carter had a control on her like you would not have believed. You would have thought by now after being married forty years the poor lady could speak her mind. She had no say so in her own life and was like a prisoner in her own home. She never had a job outside the house and Mr. Carter wanted her home all the time. She had never driven a car in her life. And there were no buses where we lived.

When Mrs. Carter needed groceries, she would walk pushing her shopping cart to the nearest store, which was ten miles round trip. She has a nice outlook on life, and she never complained about the long walk. I believe it was because she was happy to just get out of that house before she gets crazy.

Mr. Carter was the opposite. He worked in a factory for the last 22 years and his favorite past times were drinking and gambling. He is a horribly abusive drinker, and anytime Mrs. Carter would state her opinion or disagree with him, he would just beat her. One time I came home from school instead of going straight to the library, my second home I liked to call it and Mrs. Carter was crying in the kitchen, which was a sign that Mr. Carter had beaten her again. I hugged her and asked her what happened. I could see her right eye swollen as she lifted her head from the table. It was black and blue and bleeding.

Let me get you some ice.

Thank you son.

Tears came running down my face. I was so upset and pissed and knew something had to be done.

Please don't tell me you tripped and fell again, that story is getting old. Mr. Carter cannot keep on doing this to you, we need to stop him. I pleaded

How would we do that Tim? If I call the police on him after they leave he will just get angry and beat me again it would just make matter worse.

I will think of a way to stop him from doing this again. It's just not right.

Thank you Tim you are a kind boy.

Mr. Carter had two bad strikes against him. He is a mean alcoholic and he is bipolar, and he was out of control. He was always very moody and unhappy person. He bitched and complained about everyone and everything he is always negative. Mr. Carter would never take his medication he would just drink his beer instead. He was only nice to people when he wanted something from them. Not many people liked Mr. Carter. It seemed he only had one friend he chummed around with and his name was Mr. Tops. I never knew his first name and I really didn't want to know.. He was like Mr. Carter, never happy. He loved to bitch about this or that a very unhappy person.

Mr. Tops thought he was better than everyone else. The man was such a liar and a hypocrite. He would go to church on Sundays, then preach about the bible on Mondays, then screw over his co-workers or people he dealt with during the rest of the week. He had no friends, just Mr. Carter and the two were made for each other.

Mr. Tops would come by the house usually on a Friday after work, and I'd see him drink a whole twelve pack of beer, and then he would drive home. When I was home with Mr. Carter, he would always be yelling and bitching at me for no reason. He would always put me down especially in front of other people. He was very sarcastic and rude to all my friends in fact they never wanted to come over to the house anymore because of him. I remember many times when my friends were picking me up to go out, they would ring the bell or knock hard on the door and then run fast off the porch, and wait for me on the walkway. They didn't want to see or hear Mr. Carter when he opened the door. The only time he was ever nice to me was when Mrs. Turner from Kids Youth Services, would come to the house to check up on me. Mr. Carter was like an actor and he had his role down to a science. His timing was just right and was always polite with his smile that you never see otherwise. This man should be in Hollywood!

The last time Mrs. Turner came to visit, Mr. Carter would ask me how school was in front of her as if he actually cared. He would pat me on the back, smile a lot and ask questions about my friends. Another great line was Tim we need to go shopping and get you some new clothes son, you're growing so fast. Mrs. Carter would just sit there staring down at the floor with a disgusted look on her face, knowing he was full of it. Poor Mrs. Carter wanted to say something to Mrs. Turner so bad, but she couldn't. She didn't want to make Mr. Carter angry, she knew what would happen if she did, he was so full of crap she was just sick of him.

Well I'm glad to see that everything is fine here Mrs. Turner said. Tim, I'm happy that you're here with a good family – Wow. Its 4:30 already? I'm running late, I have to go. I have one more family to visit; it was good to see you guys.

Excuse me Mrs. Turner. I quickly said.

Yes, Tim?

Can I please talk to you outside just for a minute?

Tim, Mrs. Turner is running late, next time she comes back, you can talk to her when she has more time. Mr. Carter, oh-so politely said.

Oh, Louie, that's nice of you its okay. Sure Tim, let's go outside.

I walked with Mrs. Turner outside to her car. I filled her in on everything that was going on here and how Mr. Carter really is. He is like a credit card, full of plastic and out for the money.

Please, help me I begged her. I want to get out of here so bad.

Tim, I will see what I can do.

Thank you I said, feeling relieved that maybe something could be done.

Oh, Tim I wanted to ask, why was Jane wearing sun glasses in the house? Did she just have eye surgery? I called her last week and she never told me about her eye surgery. Is she ok?

I turned to look up at the house, and then turned back to Mrs. Turner, No, I said quietly. Mr. Carter hit her last week and gave her a black eye.

She was surprised. No way, Louie did that to her?

I'm going to talk to Jane tomorrow. I can't believe that Louie is such an animal.

Oh, but he is a big one I said quietly.

As I was talking to Mrs. Turner, we both looked over at the house. Mr. Carter had the window cracked open a little. We could tell he was standing on the side of the window trying to listen to our conversation. The living room curtain was pushed back so he could watch us, not aware that his fat stomach was sticking out. Mrs. Turner and I were both laughing so hard it was so funny.

You know Mrs. Turner, the eight hundred dollar a month check he receives is supposed to be for my care, and I never get a penny of it. Look at my clothes. They're old and torn and I have blisters on my toes from the sneakers I wear every day. I outgrew them months ago, and they're just too small. He won't buy me a new one.

That cheap old fart, she said I laughed at the way she said that with her southern accent. Tim, hang in there. I'm going to have a talk with him, and things are going to change trust me.

Mrs. Turner, did you know that Mr. Carter spends the money at the dog track? He loves to bet down there, and he always spending money on beer and when Mrs. Carter had asked him for money to buy me clothes, it was always the same old song the money is gone.

Between spending it all down at Jill's Bar and Grill, and betting and losing at the dog track, the money is always gone. I stopped talking when I noticed myself getting louder.

Ok Tim, I have to go, but I'm going to look into this problem and see what I can do., Thank you for telling me, have a nice day

Mrs. Turner, I'm sorry, one more thing I need to mention to you.

And what is that Tim?

I had asked Mr. Carter if he could buy me a computer so I can do my homework research, I could really use it for learning.

You got that right son, did he buy you one?

No, he said I don't need one.

I will have a have a talk with him next week, you will be getting a computer and clothes and whatever else you need, I promise you Tim.

Thank you.

Mrs. Turner, I hate living with the Carters, I want to get out of this house, it's so bad, and you have no idea what it's like to live here.

Tim, I have to go, we will talk more another time.

Ok, thank you Mrs. Turner. I stood there and watched her drive away.

CHAPTER TWO

DESERT KINGS

—◆—

M r. Carter in all reality looking back made me a smarter kid. I didn't come to that realization until later on in my life.

The local library had become my real home over time and I enjoyed the peace and quiet there. I loved to read about current affairs, the stock market was my favorite, and learning about different companies. I would spend hours reading about different stocks.

How long a company had been around, why there was a need for the product was the stock hot or not. Is there any quarterly dividend? If so, how much did it pay? How long has the CEO been with the company? What company did the CEO come from? I was so into it and wanted to learn more.

The companies that I became real interested in, I would read their profit and loss statements, and there quarterly reports. I picked out twenty two different stocks just for fun that I would watch on the library computer. I pretend to buy and sell depending on what the computer showed. I'd add up my quarterly interest, etc. But as time went on, I had also learned what I did wrong in the end. If it had been real money, I was up to ten thousand dollars at that time after I added up my quarterly interest. However, there were many times I would lose my shirt, but it was fun and very interesting learning all about the stock market.

As time had gone by, I was spending more time at the library, reading books, and working on the computer. I was really learning a lot .

Like it was yesterday, I remember when it was my turn in class to take the schools laptop home for the weekend. I got really excited walking home, thinking maybe Mr. Carter will change his mind and buy me a computer when he sees how much I could do with it. I came up with this great plan that I knew he couldn't turn away from. I would pull up a few web sites about dog racing and the history of new dogs that were coming up, and I could show him new tracks around the state and I was certain it would change his mind. Even if it meant that I would have to show the old crab about the new dogs every week, I knew it would be worth it and I had to give it a try. I figured I had nothing to lose but to gain. I had gotten myself all psyched up, ready to show him, so I decided to take a short cut home through Washington Street.

I loved walking through that back road every now and then on my way home, there were all these beautiful motorcycles with fancy paint jobs. They were fun to look at and to listen to. I'd walk slowly and hear the deep rumbling sound of the engines. It became music to my ears. Every time I'd pass by, I'd just dream of having one of those beautiful bikes of my own.

There was a bike that always caught my eye. It was this Harley soft tail; bright turquoise with purple flakes and when the sun hit the bike just right, the purple metal flakes really stood out, it was so sweet The chrome was polished so shiny that I could see my reflection. I was walking by – suddenly, two guys came flying out of the door not far from where I was walking and I jumped back, startled.

They seemed to be in a fight. I noticed they both had on the same black leather vest with big letters on the back that I could not read clearly because of the way they were moving around. I think they were in a biker club. One guy had a tattoo so big you couldn't miss it.

The artwork was unbelievable and it took up his entire right arm and shoulder. It looked like a mountain of sand in a desert with a king's crown right on top. I also noticed the big letters underneath his tattoo that read DESERT KINGS

M C and realized it was the same words on their vests. The other guy had the same mountain tattoo on the same arm, but he also had a unique tattoo on his left arm, a big colorful bobcat with face details that looked so real and under the cat in large letters read HARLEY. The two men continued yelling and cussing at each other and were jumping around and punching each other like they were in a boxing ring.

The fighting brought the men into the sidewalk, blocking right where I would have walked but I was afraid of getting hit, so I stood there just watching them. Before I knew it, the street was crowded and people were yelling and screaming as they were watching the fight. Cars that were trying to get through were slowing down and horns were blowing.

One of the guys got up from the sidewalk with blood flowing steady from the top of his head covering his face. He wiped his face with his sleeve to see where the other guy was, and then he started to charge toward him. More of the members started coming out of the same door to watch the fight, and they all were wearing that same black vest.

Watch out for the kid! A fat guy yelled out.

But he was kind of late, right as I heard him yell, I went flying. One of the guys had pushed me so hard that my books and the schools laptop went in different directions. I couldn't see where my books went, but I was able to watch the laptop. It went flying through the air and landed on a passing car, breaking right through the windshield and the driver slammed on his brakes. As I was coming down from the air, my head hit the left side, front fender of a parked car. It was a beautiful red mustang, until I put a big dent in it. My head was throbbing. My right leg hit a parking meter and I landed between the poles. My nuts were killing me! I just sat there in pain holding my leg up, cursing like crazy. When I had a moment to breathe, I suddenly heard someone yelling.

Check the boy! Make sure he's okay!

Three large men came running over to me.

Son, are you ok? One guy yelled out.

Not really! My head hurts, my leg hurts and my nuts are killing me!

We're gonna have to get you checked out. Sorry about this kid.

Yea,me too mister. I said sitting there, everything hurt and I couldn't get up.

I noticed a big bald-headed muscular man jump out of the car yelling what the hell is going on!

Someone threw this laptop at my car and broke my freaking --.

I'm sorry sir, before the man could finish his sentence, a deep loud voice yelled out, it was an accident! I will fix your car, no problem.

I want it fixed now the man screamed from across the street.

Sir don't catch an attitude with me, I'll make you part of that freaking broken windshield, Do you get my drift dude?

Just as he said that, six members of the club started walking fast over to the man's car. The man was scared. He quickly jumped back into his car and locked all the doors. Then he rolled down a window and yelled out I'm going to call the police right now!

No you won't, we don't need the cops here. Don't worry I will fix your damn car! I give you my word. You can ask any of these guys, my word is solid Dude.

Traffic was at standstill and horns were blowing. People were yelling and swearing, while this man was just arguing with the driver.

Listen Dude, he continued, I got the year, make and model of your car, come back around this time tomorrow and I'll get a new windshield in, It will take me about two hours.

He walked over to the driver car and bent down to face him.

Here is something for you, for messing up your day and I could see him hand the guy a clean hundred dollar bill, then he said my name is Duke Singer.

Thank you, the driver said as he took the bill.

And I will see you tomorrow. Duke replied, as the man drove off.

The street was getting more and more crowded and the cars were driving slowly. Some stopped just to see what was going on. Cars were stopped on the street for two blocks, what a mess. I was carried up from the hill by this large guy I later learned was named Tiny, and he was carrying me over to this other big guy named Duke.

Duke, Duke this woman called out as she was running up the hill toward him.

Hey Doc he shouted back, Can you help me?

Sure, let me call my work to let them know I'll be running late.

Can I use your phone? Mine had died.

Sure, here.

Thanks.

Tiny, take this boy in the house, Doctor will check out him out.

Ok boss! Tiny replied back, I just heard the sirens, the cops are on their way.

Tiny carried me inside and my head hurt so bad I wasn't even paying attention to who was around, but I could hear Dukes deep voice talking to the guys who were fighting.

Dudes there's no need for this behavior, what you both did was wrong, I don't care which one of you started it, you both could have handled this without fighting, I will deal with you two later, get the hell out of here now before the pigs get you both, and Bob, you better go get checked out, your head is bleeding bad dude, can you even drive?

Yea I am good.

Within ten minutes, the cops were there clearing the street out fast, then I heard a loud bang on the door.

Come in! Duke yelled in response.

Officer Mike Davis, how are you doing? What brings you here? Let me guess? Someone in the neighbor is complaining the bikes are too loud.

Not this time, I'm hearing about a fight going on down here with some of your boys.

I'm sorry that you and the guys had to come down here just for that, but they took off. I'll be sure to handle this problem when I see them both.

Then Officer Davis turned and saw me waiting for the doctor. He asked Duke what happened and if I was okay. Duke told him the situation and that the doc was treating me and that everything was cool. Then the doctor walked into the room and she greeted the officer with a smile. He smiled back and nodded his head.

Duke was a smooth talker, and he quickly changed the subject.

How's that bike of yours been running? Duke asked Officer Davis.

My bikes been down, the drive belt snapped about a month ago, I just haven't had the extra money to get it fixed.

What happened?

I was going 60 mph down Park Road, and heard a loud snap. The drive belt broke and went into the belt guard and the back wheel and jammed the bike. The bike stopped so fast I didn't see it coming and I went flying off the bike, broke two fingers on my right hand and twisted my right ankle.

Damn. Yea, Thank God for the crash bar, it saved my bike. There was only a little dent on the tank and back fender.

Then all of a sudden two other officers came in the room. Excuse me, Officer Davis all traffic is set we are out of here.

We are all going to Katie's coffee shop.

Alright I'll see you guys there in a little while, Oh Detective Nelson, don't worry about the paper work. I will take care of it when I get in the office.

Thanks Davis, I hate that freaking new computer!

Later guys! Then the detectives left.

Duke turned to Officer Davis and said I have an extra used drive belt with about 20,000 miles it is still good there is a lot of rubber on it left.

How many miles can you get on a drive belt? Officer Davis asked Duke.

The average miles are about 50,000, Tiny just reached 65,000 miles he changed his drive belt last week. We all were shocked he got that many miles on it. You're welcome to have the belt. Bring your bike here Wednesday night and leave it with me. Plan to pick up the bike Thursday after 6pm. I will put the drive belt on at no cost.

I will see you then, sounds good, thanks Duke, Oh and, by the way I will fix the report so you won't have a problem. Sergeant told all of us the next time any of us get a call to come out here again there is going to be some arrest made.

Thanks, it will never happen again I promise you.

Ok, later Duke

Officer Davis had left, and the doctor came into the room and said, Hey Duke I need to take Tim with me to the clinic to check his head and leg out better. I need to take x-rays of both, he may have a fracture. I grabbed some ice and put it on the bump that is on his head for now.

Ok doctor, Thank You!

Then Duke turned to face me, while I was holding the ice on my head.

Son my name is Duke Singer, I'm really sorry and I promise son I will make it up to you.

I'm ok Duke. I replied.

I just want to make sure. The doctor had asked Duke to pick me up and bring me home after she was finished with me, because she had other work to do. Duke without hesitation answered, Sure doctor that sounds good!

CHAPTER THREE

WELCOME TO OUR CLUB
=⟫=

T he next morning, I heard a familiar rumbling. It was a motorcycle outside pulling into the driveway. Then there was a knock on the door, followed by voices in the downstairs hallway.

Good Morning, My name is Duke Singer I am a friend of Tim.

I'm Mrs. Carter come in I will call Tim to let him know you're here.

Thank you, I'm sorry about what happened yesterday, it was a bad day.

I just got off the phone with the doctor this morning. She told me the x-rays were good, Tim had a bad sprain on his leg but nothing broken, and his head has no fractures.

Well that is good news, Thank God.

Tim you have company son. It's a gentleman name Duke

I will be right down I'm just brushing my teeth.

Duke, come into the kitchen I made some fresh coffee, would you like a cup?

Sure that sounds good, thanks.

Hey Duke what's going on?

Well, I stopped by to see how you are feeling and wanted to give you this. He said as he handed me two boxes.

One is for your school and the other is for you, I'm sorry about yesterday.

No problem Duke.

How is your leg and head?

My head is okay, the swelling went down, my leg still hurts and I can't wait to get this brace off, but I'm doing alright.

I quickly opened up the boxes, there's held a computer in each and they were much nicer than the one that flew into the car.

Damn, these are nice computers, you didn't have to buy two. Thank you so much.

I was excited to have my own computer finally.

You're welcome, Lets go, I will take you to school if that's okay with you Mrs. Carter?

Sure go ahead.

I will pick Tim up then drop him off to school until the brace is off and if for some reason I can't come by, I will send one of my guys over to get him.

Thank You Duke, for looking out for Tim, He is such a great kid and I love that boy.

It was from that day on, Duke and I developed a bond that was strong and never broke. As we pulled into the school parking lot, all the kids would watch us on the bike. I knew I would be talk of the school today. It was great to have the attention. I got off the bike and thanked him.

Oh Tim, tell me something, why was Mrs. Carter wearing sunglasses in the house at 7:00am? Boy there is something wrong with that picture.

Duke had the same tone of voice and look on his face as the one he when he had words with the guy about the windshield. Then I told Duke about how Mr. Carter treated Mrs. Carter. Duke had assured me that this problem would be taken care of.

It was only a few nights later Mr. Carter was down at Jill's bar getting drunk as usual, and when he left the bar he never made it to his car. He was jumped, beaten and robbed. They took his wallet and everything in it. Mr. Red, the bar owner, closed the bar at 1:00 am, he had to walk through some taller grass to get to his car and he tripped over Mr. Carter who had been still laying there, he was passed out and bleeding badly.

Mr. Red had called the police, and the ambulance took Mr. Carter to the hospital. The next day the news hit all the newspapers and every news station on the television. Mr. Carter told the police in his report that he didn't see who did this to him. All he could remember was hearing a lot of loud noises like motorcycles leaving before he had passed out. Thank God there were no witnesses. After hearing about his statement I knew who it was.

The next day after school I was waiting in the parking lot for Duke to pick me up. But instead, it was the same big guy that carried me the day of my accident. He showed up on his bike and introduced himself as Tiny. We talked in the parking lot for a while before I got on his bike and left. He was Duke's right hand man. I asked Tiny if we could go to the club house before he took me home. I wanted to talk to Duke so we did.

Duke was just finishing up a meeting when we walked in. He introduced me to all the members. I shook their hands and I started talking to many of the members getting to know them. It was easy to remember their names. They all had their names on the left side top of their vest. Many of the guys use a nickname.

Hey Tim, How's it going?

Good Duke, Can I talk to you?

Sure, come in my office.

Duke, thanks for helping me out with Mr. Carter. You got it bud.

Tim, I had talked to my friend Lisa who is a nurse, at the same hospital where Mr. Carter is. She gave me the low down on how that low life was doing. Mr. Carter is recovering. She started to laugh when she got to the part that he looks like a raccoon. He has not one but two black eyes.

Tim this is for you!

Duke handed me an envelope with three hundred dollars in it. This money was in Mr. Carter's wallet. What I want is for you to take the money, and go clothes shopping. You can buy whatever you need, until you run out of money. If anyone should ask where you got the clothes or the money to buy them, tell them that I bought them for you. If they have any more questions tell them to call me. I will tell them it's none of their freaking business.

The rest of the wallet, like his credit cards and license, will mail back to him.

Tim, Rusty will pick you up tomorrow afternoon when school is out. He will be waiting in the parking lot.

Cool.

He just bought a new silver Ram truck 1500. It's sweet.

That sounds good Duke.

Tim you're going to see a change in Mr. Carter, if not let me know, I will have to pay him another visit.

Ok Duke, Thanks again for your help.

By age 14, life was tough and very confusing for me. I still had a bad attitude and felt sorry for myself. I started to hang around a friend of mine Glen Perkins. He showed me the ropes on making fast money by dealing dope. The last time I went to the club house, Duke told me he was seeing a change in me and he didn't like it. He told me Mrs. Carter called him and asked if I was there hanging with him and the guys, because I was never home, and when I did come home, it was late at night.

If I wasn't dealing that night I was most likely using. I was high as a kite and I loved my pot. Once in a while, I enjoyed doing some coke but I was lucky to stay away from the hard drugs.

One evening, at about 7:00pm on a Friday night, I was hanging out on Lewis Street at the corner store parking lot where I handled the drugs, next to a gun supplier and a pimp, we all got along but dealt with business separately.

A car had pulled up with three guys and one asked me for an ounce of pot. I handed the guy in the driver seat what he asked for and he handed me the money slowly, at the same time, while the other two guys came out from the car fast. I was screwed. The driver had the drugs and I was out of a lot of cash, I just had a bad feeling that I was about to get my ass kicked. So I ran quickly and just as I reached the corner of the store, I was thinking man I did it I had gotten away! But just then, one of the guys jumped from the top of the store roof and landed right on me. I hit the ground while the other guy sat on my back and handcuffed me.

Neither of these guys said a word. They just looked at each other at different times to see what the other man was doing. They both seemed to have done this routine many times before. The driver pulled the car over and both guys picked me up from the ground and shoved me into the backseat of the car. My nose would not stop bleeding, my shirt was full of blood and all I was thinking was dam my life was over.

The car drove under a bridge on a dirt road. I started to get real nervous I begin to pray, and then the car stopped. The guy in the back seat got out of the car and tried pulling me out. I struggled and started kicking hard and I got him right in the face with my foot, and left a big shoe mark. I could tell it hurt, and he was pissed. He was swearing at me as he made a fist and right as he was about to punch me in the face, the other guy grabbed him and said don't you touch him or you will pay for that later.

Then they grabbed my feet, and jerked me out of the car as my face hit the ground. They both grabbed my feet, twisted my body over and I was now on my back as they dragged me about 30 feet and laid me under an oak tree.

I was still handcuffed from the back, and they had put on ankle cuffs on as well. Then one of the guys threw the same bag of pot that I sold to him onto my stomach and both guys ran back to the car and took off.

I was getting scared. It was pitch black out and I couldn't see anything. A few hours later, a police car was driving slowly toward me. I couldn't believe what I was seeing. Why would a cop come down here? The car drove towards me with his bright lights blinding me. I could not see anything. I heard a car door slam and then a loud voice yelled.

Well what do we have here? Tim Ripple what's going on here and what's that next to your stomach? It looks like some pot to me. You're looking at five years in prison my friend.

Someone cuffed me and planted the pot sir! I pleaded.

Now why would somebody do that?

Could you please shut your lights off sir? My eyes are killing me and I can't see.

Okay, kill the lights! He yelled out which meant there was someone else in his car. I was trying to get my vision back when I heard three doors slam. I looked up to see who else was there, but I was not able to see a thing. All I could see was a glare and I could not tell who was walking towards me.

Tim, what's going on? Don't give me the same bullshit story you just told Officer Davis! You know I can't stand people that lie, and I don't play that game.

Duke, Can you please take these cuffs off of me?

GARY M. ALLEN SR.

John, take the cuffs off of Tim.

Yes, boss.

I looked over was to see who this John guy was. My vision was getting clear, and I noticed it was one of the guys who dragged my ass out of the car handcuffed me, and threw the dope on me and took off.

I told you, no more dealing or you were going to end up in the slammer! Duke yelled at me.

Tim, if Officer Davis hadn't told me about the bust. He would have put you up with the rest of those clowns and hauled your ass off to jail like he just did to them. This is the last straw, what you do after today is up to you. I am through babysitting your ass. Life is what you make it son, stop wasting it, and feeling sorry for yourself. Get over it. It's time for you to get your shit together. Officer Davis will not arrest you this time, but if there's ever a next time he will.

I was listening to everything Duke said, and as much as I'm stubborn he is right.

Tim, these three guys are new members so forget what happened and let's start over. Don't catch an attitude with them. I told them to do it. This is John, Rob, and Don.

John spoke up, Tim we regret what happened to you and we're sorry, we were just following the boss's orders. Let's all be friends.

Then we all shook hands, apologized for the fighting, and I told Duke and the guys that I was done for good, no more dealing or using. The guys invited me back to the club house for a few beers,

Can I fit in the car?

Officer Davis replied, sure just don't let the cops see all of us in this car. Then we all laughed.

A few weeks later, I decided to swing by the clubhouse to talk to Duke. I walked in and started talking with a few of the club members while they were shooting pool. Then I knocked on Dukes office door and he yelled out come on in.

Hey Duke

Hey Tim, how's it going?

Not bad Duke, but I have a little problem, I was wondering if you could help me out.

Sure, I'm all ears, what's up?

Well, the school wants us to do a fund raiser because they need to raise money to buy new books for the students. With the state cutting back, and the schools not getting as much tax money as they used too, the economy is so bad here in Detroit.

I persuaded the class to do a bake sale along with a carwash on the same day. I figured maybe if one idea doesn't work the other will. Or hopefully they both will make money.

Sounds good Tim.

And Duke, I was wondering if you and the guys would help us out and come for a bike wash at the school. It is in two weeks on a Saturday.

Sure, we will be there. Thanks again, I got to go, see you later.

Wait Tim, I need your help.

Sure what can I do?

There are two members who have a court order against them, forbidding them to see their kids until things are straightened out. We both know how the court system is so damn slow. I believe the guy's two kids go to the same school as you, maybe a different grade, I'm not sure.

Could you find them and mention to them that their fathers will be at the carwash, and would love to see them?

Sure Duke, I can do that.

Tim, you have to tell these two kids that no one can know about them coming to meet them, especially their mothers, these guys will end up in the county jail if they get caught breaking the restraining order.

I got you. Sure I will tell them.

Then Duke handed me a folded up paper with the names of the boys on it. I told him I would take care of it. Thank you Tim, and tell Mrs. Carter to call me, I will take her to the hospital and pick her up, I know she needs a ride to visit him

That's nice of you Duke, I will tell her.

Tim it's the least I could do after kicking her husband ass. He said, and then he laughed.

Weeks later I was working at the schools car wash. It was a hot, muggy, cloudy day, and it looked like it was going to down pour. My classmates and I were two hours in, and only eight cars had come through, business was very bad. Then one of the teachers came over to tell us and said in 15 minutes, we were going to pack it in for the day, because it was just too slow. Not too long after he said that, I heard loud rumbling noises, there was Officer Davis in the cop car with the lights flashing leading Duke and all the other guys. I watched, and counted 25 motorcycles coming down the street. What a nice sound and sight to see all the different colors and custom choppers all lining up to get their bikes washed.

You could tell by the looks on their faces that some of the parents and teachers and seemed afraid of the club members. So I broke the ice and introduced Duke and the members to all the faculty there and friends. It was really a big happy party, most of the members had kids in that school, and so they were able to spend some time with them and their teachers.

The profit from the car wash was $200 and the profit from the bake sale was $100, and on top of it all the proceeds, the club members donated $500 to help the school out. Everyone was thrilled.

That Monday afternoon I was in class when the classroom phone rang. Principal Mr. Adams needs to see you now Tim my teacher told me. When I got to his office, he shook my hand and thanked me for what I did at the wash. He also asked me how I met Duke and the club members. I could tell he was concerned but I explained to him that Duke and the guys were my family and that they all look out after me. Mr. Adams shook his head I see Tim. Well please tell them all that I said thank you for helping us out. Now we will be able to get our new books, thanks to the club.

I definitely will tell them today I'm going to see them after school. Ok Tim have a nice day.

After school was out, I headed to the clubhouse. Many of the club members thanked me, and mentioned how they were happy to be there at the car wash, and to spend time with their kids and meeting the teachers. Dick and Ted thanked me for talking to their kids about coming to the car wash. They both haven't seen their kids for six months, so it worked out great. Then they both told me whatever I wanted, I would get. I asked Ted if he could give me guitar lessons, I had always wanted to learn to play.

Ted told Dick, and so Dick bought me a nice new guitar, I was in heaven. Ted was the manager and owner of the top rock and roll band in Detroit, they were called {The Up Beats}. Every Thursdays after school, I started getting together with Ted at his ice cream shop down the street from the school. He would give me lessons and I eventually joined in with his bands practice after I got really good. It was a lot of fun.

A year had gone by, and I remember it was a Saturday night at eight o'clock. Dick came over to my house to ask Mrs. Carter if it was okay that he took me to see Duke because he needed to talk to me.

Sure she said that's alright, and could you take these chocolate chip cookies I made and give them to Duke for me?

Yes I will. Dick told her.

Thank you, see you guys later and we left.

So Dick what does Duke want to see me about?

You are going to play with the band tonight at the Golden Glass Night Club down town.

Dick. I'm under age I can't get in the club, there's no way.

Do you want to bet?

You must know something I don't.

Got that right Tim. Rusty bought the night club last week.

Wow! that's cool.

When we walked into the club, all the members and customers were yelling out my name.

Hey Tim.

Are you ready to jam with the band?

Yes Ted.

Let's go.

What a blast, we had so much fun, and everyone loved us. A few weeks later I had stopped in the club house.

Hey, Duke, how's it going?

Good Tim

Duke, I want to repay you for helping me out I really appreciated it.

Tim, just keep doing well in school and stay out of trouble. That's all I would like you to do for me.

Okay Duke. I have a way to make the club money.

Let's hear it son. I am all ears talk to me.

I can help you and guys make money on the stock market, I will be your Broker I will buy and sell stocks for you guys.

I showed him on my computer how it works and the stocks that had made money. Tim I'm impressed! Duke said to me. I told him I've spent many hours reading and learning about stocks at the library. And it paid off.

Ok, Tim. It sounds good! I'm sure the guys will love to do it. It's a great way to make some money. How much money will we need to start?

Fifteen hundred will be good.

Duke here is all the paperwork I picked up at the brokers office. I talked to a man name Charles Leaf and I told him that it's for you and he said you will need to call him for appointment with him. Here is his card, sounds good Tim.

And can you make the check out to the company Your -Trade.

Sure Tim, I will start the account with two thousand dollars and I will fill out the paperwork that we need now. Do you have a few minutes?

Sure Duke then Tim I will drop it off to Charles then you can start investing for us.

Chapter Four

Reality is Setting In

The last few months were tough, having to watch Mrs. Carter slowly facing death as the cancer got worse. I had been helping her out as much as I could after school. Duke would pick Mrs. Carter up and drive her to the doctor office for her chemo sessions. One day, I was at the house helping Mrs Carter cook and prepare dinner and Mrs. Turner came by to visit and see how she was doing.

As Mrs. Turner was leaving, she asked me to walk out to her car because she wanted to talk to me. She told me that it was up to me to decide who I wanted to live with, when Mrs. Carter passed away, which could be any time now. She had handed me information on each of the three families that wanted to foster me. I read all the information and decided what family I wanted, so I contacted the Whites. I sent out an email to Mr. and Mrs. White and introduced myself they were very surprised and happy that I had contacted them. For a few months, we conversed back and forth and I got to know more about who they were. A few years back, they had lost their son Johnny in an auto accident. They seemed to be very nice people and down to earth.

The time was here Mrs. Carter was sent to hospice. I was there visiting her after school, keeping her company, when her husband, Mr. Personality came to visit her. I had left and headed for home. I could tell by our conversation that Mrs. Carter was worried about the medical bills. The insurance sucked, it hardly covered anything. So I talked to Duke about it.

Duke and the guys decided to help her out. The club did a poker run to raise money up for her hospital bills. There were a hundred and fifty bikers in the poker run and they were from other clubs, which Duke and the guys were good friends with. A few weeks later, Duke came over to the hospital to visit and gave Mrs. Carter a check for ten thousand dollars. She was so happy she just could not stop thanking him for all his help and for the money.

Five weeks later, the sad day came and Mrs. Carter had passed away. I was staying with Duke and the guys that night. The next few days we all went to her service. Not only was I upset losing her but I was also pissed that Mr. Carter never showed up for her service. I stayed around another week, to tie things up before I head to Connecticut and move in with the Whites. It was tough to go and I will miss Duke and the member's.

I grabbed my suitcase and walked out the front door, heading for the taxi that was in the driveway blowing the horn. The cabbie drove me to the club house. I will get a ride to the airport from here, thank you. I said to him.

Are you sure young man?

Oh, it's ok, my friends will take me. Sir, keep the change as I tipped him five dollars.

Thank you son He said as he grabbed the money from my hand. Then he looked up at me with a shocked look on his face. You know son, it's none of my business, but those gang members, Desert Kings, are crazy! Son, you know you can get hurt going in there.

I thank you for your concern, but those guys are my friend's. Duke, the President of the club, is like my Godfather.

Ok son that's cool, Then you're all set young man.

Carl, one of the members, walked out of the club house and lit up a cigarette. He looked at me leaning on the cab talking to the cabbie. He yelled out to me as the smoke was coming out of his mouth. Hey Tim is everything ok?

Oh yea, I'm just talking to the cabbie.

You should get your ass inside, they're waiting for you.

Ok son, you have a nice day and may God bless and watch out for you, thank you for the tip, the driver said once again before he drove off.

Tears were rolling down my face. I could just not stop thinking about how reality was setting in. I was leaving these guys, they were my family. At first, I hated having to move here and the changes. But it was them Duke and the guys who helped me deal with all of it. To my surprise, not only were there all the club members at my party, but also my friends were there, a few of my favorite teachers, and of course the Principal Mr. Adams. It was nice to see them.

Tim, we have a surprise for you! Duke shouted to me.

What's that Duke?

Ricky is going to give you a club tattoo.

Seriously? That's great! Thank you.

Everyone grab your beer.

Than Duke yelled out Tim here then he handed me a cold beer.

Thanks

Lets all make toast here's to the youngest member Tim Ripple. We are all going to miss you man. We wish you well with your new family and you know our door is always open if you need any of us, just call or text us anytime. Cheers.

Hey boss, there's a cop car that just pulled into the driveway. Dave, look to see who it is.

What is the number of the car?

It's 23.

It's Officer Davis, I had invited him, let that boy in.

You got it boss.

Officer Davis walked in. Hey guys, how's it going?

Great, come on in Duke shouted back.

Officer Davis walked right up to me. Hey Tim, this is for you, and he handed me an envelope, Good luck in your new home.

Thank you, I said to him, I'm really going to miss everybody.

Have some cake and coffee Officer Davis.

Thanks Duke, but I'd rather have a cold beer like the one Tim is drinking. He replied with a laugh. Hey Duke, I didn't know the state changed the law for drinking, and tattooing from the age 21 to 16. It's amazing what you can do in a club house behind closed doors. Then we all started laughing.

Hey Officer Davis, this is for you. Duke said as he handed him a cold one.

Thanks Duke.

The party is ending, and I had to leave to catch my plane. Everyone had lined up to shake my hand, and some handed me more envelopes of money. I said my goodbyes to everyone and left with Tiny and Duke who drove me to the airport. As the plane was taking off, I waved down at them as their bikes drove away from the airport with what looked like to me their thumbs were up.

Everything looked so different from the plane, in the air the city's seemed so small, and I found myself staring at the clouds thinking about everything I had been through.

If there was one person that I looked up to, it was Duke Singer. I wanted to be just like him. He was very smart, well liked, a smooth talking ladies' man, and he always went out of his way to help others out. He did so much for me, and really helped me changed my life around. He was never afraid to take charge with anything in his life. I remembered what Tiny told me about Duke. That he once told Rusty and him that if he made it home alive from Afghanistan there were two things he would be sure to do. The first was to leave the police department; he was tired of being a cop. He wanted to start his own investigating company, which he successfully did and now has five people work from him. The second was to simply buy a brand new bike and ride. And that's exactly what he did. I'm sure going to miss Saturday mornings, watching those beautiful bikes screaming as they pull out of Washington Street.

Before Duke moved in that neighborhood on Washington Street there was a lot of crime. It was the bad side of town, from drugs, prostitution, shootings, human trafficking, and gangs. Duke bought three abandoned homes they all had three floors. He just walked into the bank and told the bank manager that he would like to buy the three houses for fifteen thousand dollars. The manager called him up a few days later and told him he had a deal. So Duke bought them. The houses needed a lot of work too, but he didn't care, he took his time and fixed them up. The banks had repossession on all the property on Washington Street because of default loans. The crime was so bad, that property owners would just walked away from the property so the bank ended up taking the property's back. The banks were sitting on some properties for over five years, they were happy to unload them. Even the cops didn't like to go there, when they were called out to that neighborhood the chief would always have two officers in one police car and he would send three cruisers on every call they received.

Duke got rid of one bad group at a time. The loco street gang that lived down the street from him they became good friends with Duke and the other members. They helped him out with cleaning up the neighborhood. Duke got rid of the drug dealers, and pimps by simply asking them to leave, which of course they refused. So Duke and the guys just blew up three of their cars. When all the commotion was over, the pimps and the drug dealers had left the neighborhood fast for good. They knew now that Duke was crazy wasn't playing around.

The police had a feeling Duke had something to do with the car explosions but never pursued the case, they were happy the hood was getting cleaned up.

Duke and the guys got rid of the human trafficking issue, by setting up the owners of that organization. The police raided homes made many arrests, and put all the poor kids into family care.

Duke asked Tiny and Rusty for help rebuilding the homes and in return, they got to stay rent free, and eventually Duke gave them both ownership of one of the floors on the three family homes. The houses were the best looking ones on the street, and Duke decided to turn the bottom floor to one of the homes into a club house. Six months later Duke, Tiny and Rusty started the club. Within a year there were twelve members and the whole neighbor was practically crime free.

A year later, the Sunday's newspaper had a nice article mentioning Duke and the club members and how they changed the neighborhood. The article mentioned that Duke is giving free rent to the Battered Woman Association. The women felt safe knowing that Duke and the members were next door. And in return, the women would bake the member's treats and cakes and even cleaned the club house once a week.

Duke was always a gentleman. He was like their older brother, although a few of the ladies you could tell by the way some of them looked and talked to Duke it was so obvious they wanted more. He made a club rule that no member could ever get involve with any of the ladies in the shelter if so they would be thrown out of the club. After that review from the paper talked about how beautiful Washington Street was getting. Investors were starting to buy up the abandoned property, down from Dukes houses fixing them up and renting them out.

Through the last few years hanging out with them, I found out that Duke, Tiny, and Rusty were old school friends. In fact, Tiny used to tell me stories now and then about the three of them in the army together, and when they went overseas to Afghanistan. Rusty took out one of the two bullets out of Dukes right leg in a foxhole while they were fighting. He had taken an old rusty can he found in the dirt, and cut it open. Then he ripped his shirt and wrapped it around Dukes leg he used the can to hold it in place. Then with his belt, he strapped it around the can to stop the bleeding.

Rusty told me that if they operated and try to take out the other bullet there would be an 80% chance that Duke would lose that leg. So Duke he just dealt with the pain that why he walks with a limps.

All of a sudden I heard the wheels from the plane come out from underneath and within minutes we hit the ground into Bradley's Airport. I got off the plane and I went straight for my luggage. As I was taking my bags off of the conveyor belt, I heard a loud voice yell out. Tim is that you son?

Betty and Joe White were waiting for me, and I walked over and gave them both hugs. We started talking about so much, laughing when we cut each other off because we were all just so happy to see each other. The Whites lived in a small country town in Connecticut called Rocky Hill. Acres and acres of farmland cows were all over. It took me a while to get used to. I was use to the city.

The Whites and I were getting acquainted over phone calls and through emails for over a year. We were trying to get to know each other better and thank God it worked. I felt very comfortable with them, and felt like I really had a set of parents that cared for me this time. Nothing like it's been in the past. They were both very nice and down to earth people. A few days later, they took me out to dinner at their favorite steak restaurant in town on the Silas Dean Highway. They told me about the sad story of their son Johnny. He was my age, and he had been killed in a car crash five years ago. Linda Star, his girlfriend was with him and was lucky enough to survive the crash. The doctors didn't think she was going to pull through, in fact her father called the family priest to give Linda her last rights. The poor girl was hospitalized for eighteen months. The doctor has to amputate her left leg she now has a prosthetic, light-weight, fiberglass, flesh colored leg. You'd never know the leg was not real.

The accident happened on a cold, dark, sleeting December night, about 11:00 pm. Johnny was driving Linda home from the movies, when a car ran a red light on Elm Street, and came into their lane. They were side swiped at 85 miles an hour, in a 40mph zone. Johnny lost control of his car and it flipped twice. They later learned that Johnny and Linda were hit by an underage kid named Mark Heal, who apparently came from money. His grandfather was very well known in the court system as Judge Bailey. So he had a lot of pull in the state.

The night of the accident, Marks parents were on vacation on a cruise ship. Mark decided to take his father's 560 SL Mercedes Benz to a party and was liquored up. Mark got away with murder. Mrs White said life is not fair. It's not what you know it's who you know.

Mark lost his license for six months. He paid a fine of $2,000, and did three months of community service and didn't have to do any jail time. He got away with everything. Johnny is dead, Linda lost a leg.

I could tell the Whites were upset that this kid Mark Heal was completely free, thanks to their grandpa Judge Bailey and I couldn't blame them, and I'd be pissed too. Both families, the Whites and the Stars, still have a lawsuit pending against Mark. They have been in and out of court for over four years, fighting for the lawsuit and no luck yet.

I still remembered the time I came home from school late at night, and was heading to my bedroom to get some sleep, when I noticed Mrs. White in the living room. She was holding her son Johnny's photos in her hand, crying so hard that Mr. White ran into the room and hugged her. He would talk to her and calm her down but by the time he walked her out of the room, he would also be crying. I felt so sorry for them both, that Johnny was no longer here, and tears were still flowing years later. It must be devastating to have a child die before the parents. I am like many people, hoping God takes us the parent first before them the child.

Mr. White was not only like a father to me he also became my best friend. He would come to all my school activities and support me. I will never forget the time when I was playing basketball on the school team. We were playing for the state championship. The gym was packed, and all the seats in the bleachers were taken. People were standing everywhere to see this game. We even had the Press and TV coverage. There were twenty-two seconds left in the game, and it was a tied score. In the last quarter, our team got the ball as we ran down the court and kept passing the ball to each other to stall time. I was the last person to receive the ball, I had an open shot and there was only five seconds left to go before the game ended! Sweat was pouring down my face like a water faucet left on.

The pressure was on, the crowd was going crazy, yelling and screaming and banging the bleachers. Suddenly the coach started yelling, Tim, Take that shot! I took the shot at half court, I had no choice, and time was running out, I felt so confident. Then as the ball flew through the air, everyone was silent. You could hear a pin drop it was so quiet, just before the ball went into the hoop {swish!} then everyone went crazy. I heard Mr. White yelling out great job Tim! That's my boy then you could hear the slam of the ball back onto the court. Seconds later, the buzzer went off, our team had won the championship game. Mr. White was so proud of me. It made me feel so good and I could feel the love and see how much he really cared.

Time went on, and one night Johnny's best friend Tom Hill came over, he was on leave from the service. Tom loved to have a few beers and talk about old times about him and Johnny he would have Mr. White laughing. Mrs. White would have to leave the room because it still bothered her to hear about her son she missed so much. I also met

Johnny's girlfriend Linda that night. She was very close to Mrs. White, they had a mother-daughter relationship.

Linda's mother passed away from breast cancer when Linda was ten. Mr. Star raised Linda and her brother Bobby, as a single parent and he never remarried. His job was his life, being a city cop, and he loved it. A very friendly guy who would always boast about himself. He loved the attention. He would never ask me or anyone else any questions about what was going on with our lives. Like how are the Whites doing? Or Tim how's school? No, it was always about him. There were times when the Whites would have a cookout and invited the Stars family and friends over. Mr. Star would talk about his work or a story about him twenty years ago, a lot of useless information but we all listened to. He just loves the center of attention. Then when people talked he would not listen. Mr. Star would always think of what story he could tell next.

Then when he was finished with what he wanted to talk about, he would fall asleep at the table. We were having coffee, dessert talking and laughing, just having a great time. Everyone at the table could tell Linda and her brother Bobby, were pissed at Mr. Star for being so rude. Linda apologized to all of us before she woke up her Dad to go home. I believed that Linda spent a lot of time with Mrs. White, going shopping, going out to lunch, or just to hanging out to get away from her father.

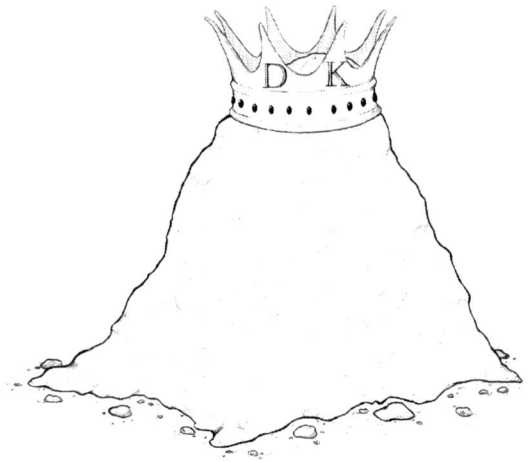

CHAPTER FIVE

TALKING TRASH

As the years went by, I stayed out of trouble and was doing well. I graduated high school, and continued my education. I was able to get my college degree, a bachelor in criminal and family law. Now I only had two more years of law school to go and pass the bar exam, and my dream will come true. To become a great and honest attorney. But a drastic change was about to happen in my life, and I wasn't prepared for. My wife wanted a divorce and I ended up dropping out of school. I never knew this was going to happen. After five years of marriage, my wife had as of roaming eyes.

One day I received a call at work from my son's babysitter. She was crying telling me my wife had taken off with her husband. No one knew where either of them where, or my son. I skipped my class, and went straight home after work. The house was empty, my wife had taken everything. At least she was nice enough to leave me one toothbrush, a blowup mattress, one frying pan, one egg, and a roll of toilet paper. Good to know she was so thoughtful. She took all of our money out of our savings account, that girl was really generous when it came to my half of everything. She took me to the cleaners, I had nothing.

I could not understand why she left. I was a good husband, and father, and family man, Sure, we had arguments like everyone else did that's normal. We had money, our sex life was good. We did a lot of things together I was just in shock, and in pain. I was still in love with her; I always thought our marriage was good there were never any signs of her being unhappy. It's funny how some people think that the grass is always greener on the other side of the fence. Until they've been there a while and see that the grass starts to get brown. Not to mention the fence needing repair, I am sure you can relate to that. I lost everything in my life. My son Peter my job, apartment, all my money.

Three days later I received a letter from my ex-wife to be with no return address on the envelope. I started to read her Dear Tim letter. The babysitter was right her husband was living with my wife, and my son Peter. Its, funny how quickly one life can change. Joan, my ex-wife mentioned how she would contact me when they settled down in their new home in Coventry. After reading her letter, it was obvious to me that these two were seeing each other for a long time. Now I know where half of my money went. The only good news was in a few weeks, she'd call me, and I could pick up Peter. Now her mystery was starting to unravel.

I just had to pick up the pieces, and start over, but that was easier said than done. Well thank God for the Whites. They were there for me again, and I was able to move back into their home until I got a job and made some money, and could get my own place. They were so excited to have me come back home.

I had lost interest in going back to school to get my law degree. I thought it would be a waste of time and money. I could not seem to concentrate and was just not in the right state of mind. I decided after some time, that it was time to change my career. I had enough with turning wrenches, and that was getting boring. I decided to go to a tractor trailer school, and after I graduated. The school had a job placement, but most of the jobs were over the road. I wanted to stay around to spend more time with Peter.

That morning, I got up early to read the paper and one article was saying that the economy in the state of Connecticut was doing well. Jobs were tough to find though, because people were staying with their positions. Unemployment was the lowest in 8 years. I came across two companies that were looking for drivers. Neither of them said you must have experience. So I took a fast shower and drove to the first company to apply. It was an oil company in East Hartford driving tankers. I walked in and asked the lady at the front desk for an application. After I filled it out, the lady said a gentleman would be with me in a minute.

Thank you I told her.

Suddenly, I heard a deep voice, Tim come into my office young man.

Yes sir.

My name is Craig Smith.

It's nice to meet you Mr. Smith.

Call me Craig, How can I help you son?

I'm applying for the driver's job you have posted in the paper. I am a good driver sir.

I'm sure you are.

I'm not afraid of work.

Tom, I mean, Tim, you have no driving *experience!* He yelled, as he threw down my application on his desk, which it then fell to the floor.

So I picked it up from the floor and handed it back to him. I'm sorry about that.

Tim, a year ago my son graduated from a culinary school, and he still can't find a job. Listen son, go out there, get some experience and then come back to see me. Then I'll be able to hire you.

As I got up from the chair, I shook Craig's hand, thanking him for the interview and started walking towards the door. I stopped when I reached the door, turned around and Craig was standing behind me. Sir, I have an important question for you.

Okay Tim.

Sir I'm not getting smart with you, I'm just asking honestly. There are companies just like this one that will not give people like your son and I the chance to get the experience we need. We all have to start somewhere right? I know someone took you in and helped you climb the ropes at one point.

I noticed Craig's face was getting red, and he was speechless for a moment, Yes, Tim, you are right. I understand what you're telling me son. Let me do this, I will talk to the owner next time when he comes here and I will try to get you in. I can't promise you a job, but I will try.

Thank you Craig, that sounds great.

I left, and drove two blocks down the road. There was a hot dog joint called Frankenstein. I had heard that this place had the best dogs in the state. They were always in the newspapers and food magazines with great reviews. I pulled in the parking lot, grabbed my paper, and sat to enjoy a great lunch. While reading the paper, I noticed the other job I wanted to apply for, gave an address but no name. However, I was in luck, the company was right around the corner from where I was. I drove down the street, and saw this beautiful building. It had very fancy bricks with tinted windows, and sat three stories high. Right above the front door was a big sign that read Automatic-Waste-Away.

I attempted to open the door, but it was locked. There was a small sign on the window of the door and I mean small you really had to look hard to see the little sign, saying please ring the bell to enter.

So I did then I heard a loud, deep voice that sounded like an older lady talk through the speakers. I jumped. It scared the crap out of me. Can I help you? The voice said.

I really didn't expect to hear a voice, just a buzzer to let me in the door. Good afternoon, I would like to apply for a driving job you had advertised in today's newspaper.

Come in take the elevator to the second floor. Off the elevator, take a right and the third door is Human resource department.

I thanked her as the buzzer went off and I pulled the door open. I walked in, and stopped for a few seconds. I could not help staring at the floor. It was white with gold specks, looked like Italian marble, and it was such a beautiful floor. I've never seen anything like it. There were four huge chandeliers that lit up when the sun hit the crystals, and you could see gorgeous rainbows all over the walls. The elevator was striking. It was clear glass all around so you could see who was riding in it. The outside of the elevator had all different colors with small flashing lights. It was sharp.

There was soft music playing, surrounding the room and in the middle of the lobby was a waterfall that had three tiers of seashell made of marble. The top sea shell had a hand carved statue of a woman with long brown hair and a smile on her face standing in front of the waterfall, holding a large fish. Water was pouring out of the fish's mouth, landing on the second seashell. The statue was so stunning the detail of the carving actually looked real. The bottom seashell was a nice big pond with different colored lights on the bottom with real plants. I looked inside the water fountain and there were large live Chinese gold fish, swimming around enjoying the water.

While I waited for the elevator to come down, I could not help noticing the detailed pictures on the wall with gold frames. All the artwork was unbelievable. It was as if you were at an art show. There was a marble table next to the waterfall filled with fresh cut roses. That nice aroma had filled the room. I felt as if I was in a casino, not a garbage company. The owners must have spent a mint building this palace. I walked over to the elevator that was coming down and saw a young man in a nice suit reading the paper. He was also waiting for the elevator. As I walked into the elevator, a loud beep startled me, and then I heard a voice say, Good afternoon Mr. Tim Ripple. And without thinking I answered back good afternoon.

The man standing behind me started laughing. Then the voice said. Good afternoon Mr. Cliff Lewis. Please check your email, you have two new messages.

My mouth just dropped open, I was in shocked. I could not believe what I had just heard. Then the man looked at me and said, it's nice to meet you Tim Ripple.

It's nice to meet you to Cliff Lewis.

Tim, I'm sorry I didn't mean to laugh, but your expression on your face was so funny. It was like something you would see on that show Kandid-Camera. Don't feel bad, it took me awhile to get use to that computer.

Damn, I can't believe the computer knows who the people are that come into the building and know all the information about them. This is mind boggling.

You got that right Tim, it sure is. The Bluetooth reads everyone's phones when they enter the building. By the time a person enters the elevator, the computer already knows their name and all their information. Then the [Your Tooth] program sends the photo of the person and all there information to Joey by email to his Y-Phone. There is a camera at the front door that you can't see.

Joey, the owner, gave all the sale people the Y-Phone. It does everything.

The Phone is so easy to work with, you can check your voice messages, emails, text messages, stocks quotes, calendar, notes, calculator, and it even has a nice camera to take photos. It has so many great apps that can help a person obtain so much knowledge.

That's neat Cliff, how did this Bluetooth come about?

Well Joey had worked out a deal with one of his customers, Art Nicholson how owns Gadget Plus. The store is on Asylum Street in Hartford, Tim have you ever been in that store?

No Cliff I haven't.

Tim have to check out he store sometime. Art has a lot of electronics devices that no one else seem to have.

Joey met with Art to sign him up for trash pickup and they started to talk. He mentioned to Joey that he needed a place to check out his own product called {Your Tooth} and get the bugs out of the program, so Art could market it. It's great for Joey he always wants to know who's is in his building all the time. Joey and Art decided to swapped services.

So Tim, what brings you here?

Oh I'm applying for a job.

I hope you get the job. I've been working here for six years now. I love this company. It's great we have the best benefits around.

Oh this is my floor. It was nice talking to you Cliff.

Same here Tim, I hope you get the job. Thanks have a nice day.

I got off the elevator I started to walk to the human resource department, when I saw a sign hanging from the wall in big letters reading WATER.

I was thirsty I just had stopped and get a drink. I walked over to the water fountain. I started to laugh I could not believe my eyes. I have seen a lot of different things in my life before, but this one takes the prize. The water fountain was made in Italy, it was a statue of a tiger faces which was the size of a basketball, the tiger was painted orange with black stripes with brown eyes and it looked so real made from porcelain.

On top of the tiger head was a little button when you pressed down the button water was shooting out of the tigers mouth. The claws were holding the round base marble where the drain was. About six feet past the fountain, was a huge Spathiphyllum plant in a big, colorful marble pot that was against the wall. There was a small black hose about 1 inch diameter that came out of the wall into the potted plant.

It was so neat, when you wanted to water the plant just run the water fountain. As I walked into the human resource a woman greeted me Hello young man, I thought you got lost on me.

Oh no I was just checking out the great view. It's so beautiful.

Your right, how did you like the water fountain?

It was neat.

She handed me an application. Have a seat over there, let me know when your finish. I will call one of the owners and they will give you an interview today.

Okay Thank You.

As I turn around, I could not help noticing the wall was filled with beautiful picture of brand new, painted dark green garbage truck. Mack trucks front-end loaders, rear end loaders. Then there was a Pete belt roll-off trucks. They even had a photo of a Mercedes truck that delivered cans to the customers. All the trucks had chrome, rims, bumpers, tail pipe. They were sharp. The name of the company in big white letters painted on the driver's side door on all the trucks Automatic -Waste-Away.

I could not help hearing two men arguing so loud from office down the hall. Both men had heavy Italian accents. One man said to the other man if he does not pick uppa the banka trash this afternoon, and get backa to the yard early, so help me I will fire that fat piece of work, and make sure he doesn't get hired anywhere. We are going to lose that account. Nicky do you remember how hard it was to get that?

Yea Joey, I sure do.

Joey calm down, your blood pressure is rising, and you face is getting red.

You are sweating you may have another heart attack.

No, I'm ok Nicky, call big bad Mackey now, tell him he is fired, if the banks are not picked up this afternoon after 4.00 the same goes for his crew no one's leaves early.

I'm finished Miss.

Okay, hold on one minute, she got on the intercom phone and yelled out, Joey this young man is here for the job?

Thank you Margaret, please send him over to me.

Yes Joey.

Young man, go out the door, take a right, two doors down on the left is Joey's office.

Thank You Margaret, have a nice day.

Thank You young man I will try. Thank God it's Friday.

She said as she started laughing.

I walked down the hallway enjoying the gorgeous view. I kept on thinking to myself I would really love to work here. That old saying, someone's trash is another ones treasure sure did apply here, this building was a perfect example of it. Just as I was going to knock on the door a loud voice yelled. Come in.

Have a seat.

Then he took my application from my hand.

Thank you.

Is it Tim or Timmy?

What name do you go by young man?

Tim, Sir

I'm Joey Mancini and this is my brother-in law Nicky Maraschino.

You can call us by our first names.

Okay gentleman, thank you.

It's nice to meet both of you.

As Joey was checking out my application, Nicky kept on checking me out, staring at me up and down as if he know me. He was very annoying.

Joey is big and fat. I would have to guess his weight is about three hundred fifty pounds. He is a tall man about six feet five inches. I'm talking about a big man. He is wearing nice dress clothes Penney loafers, just casual and a lot of Italian gold, three gold rings on each hand with different stones in them. He is wearing a gold chain on his neck with a cross and a black star sapphire stone in the middle of it. On the right hand he is wearing a thick Italian gold bracelet, on his left wrist and a beautiful presidential watch selling price was $ 17,000.00. The watch is sharp. It was the same watch that I saw in Bills jewelry store, when I went in to get a battery for my twenty five dollar watch. Joey was more into gold than clothes. He has thick black hair and goatee trimmed nice it was obvious he was younger than the other man Nicky.

Joey looked in his early forty.

Nicky I would have to say he was in his late fifty's.

He was the opposite of Joey, five feet, slim bald, big nose. He had a long big jagged deep line scar in the middle of his right side of his face. It looked like someone took a sharp knife to him. Nicky wore no jewelry. He is clean cut and is really into clothes no doubt about it. He is wearing a beautiful three piece suit, dark blue with a light blue pinstripe in it. He had on a light blue silk shirt to match the pin stripes in the suit, with a solid blue tie, and a light blue plain handkerchief in his left top suit pocket.

The suit he had on was made from silk Armani. It must have been custom tailor it fit him perfect.

To top it off Nicky wore a pair of nice light blue alligator-skin shoes that match the pin stripes in his suit. I had never seen alligator-skin shoe before, only in men's magazine. They were 400.00 dollars a pair. They were beautiful shoes. Dress for success Nicky sure was a role model for that saying. He is a sharp dresser I will give him that much credit I was very impress. The after shave he had on was so strong it smelled the whole room it smelled like spice it was so bad. It has to go it smelled gross.

Tim I see you graduate from Tractor-Trailer School a few weeks ago.

Yes, Joey I did.

You have no driving experience.

Your right Sir I do not.

I'm not afraid to work, and I'm honest. I do not mind working overtime; I will take good care of your customers and trucks.

I like your attitude son, Joey replied. Joey and Nicky both started to hammer away, taking turns asking me question.

Tim what are your goals in life?

First goal, I will finish my education get my law degree and to become the best and honest lawyer in this state. My second goal is to get custody of my son Peter. My third goal is to find the killers who murder my mother.

All of a sudden the room was quiet.

Nicky and Joey just stared at each other with their mouth open speechless, as if they saw a cat that jumped five feet in the air and caught a bird in its mouth and ate it whole. Nicky took out a handkerchief from his pants pocket to wipe off the sweat from his face. I guess what I had said, had shocked both of them. At this point now, I am wondering if I got the job or not?

All of a sudden, Joey said I am glad to hear you want to finish college and get your law degree. Do you think you can work hard all day then go to school at night son? And be here by four thirty am?

Yes, Joey I know I can do it.

Why was your mother killed Nicky asked me quickly?

Nicky don't ask Tim personal question maybe he does not want to talk about it.

Son you don't have to answer that question if you do want to.

Nicky I prefer not to talk about its sir. I could tell that Joey had a kind heart. Nicky face had a frown with a pissed off look. Nicky was another story he was just plain nosy.

I see your divorced, do you have any children.

Yes Joey,I have one son Peter he is seven. I have him on weekends.

Joey do you have any children?

Yes two, one son Tony he is about your age. He works here as a driver. He is learning the business, starting from the bottom. My daughter Carol has four children. I love those kids.

Then Nicky asked me, How mucha child support do youa pay?

I pay One Hundred Dollars a week.

What that is a lot of money a week to be dishing out.

Joey started yelling, what do you mean that is a lot of money Nicky. That is his son his own blood.

Tim speaking of blood, your nose is bleeding son. Put your head down, not back you don't want to choke on your blood. Nicky started yelling loud at Joey, to put some papers on the floor where his blood is dripping, he is messing up our beautiful rug.

Then Joey started to yell back at Nicky.

Nicky, give Tim your handkerchief the one in your top pocket in your jacket.

H E L L O no way. What are you freaking crazy?

This handkerchief had cost me too much to get blood on it.

Never mind Nicky be that freaking way.

You,cheap bastard.

Here is some tissues son.

Thanks Joey.

It should stop bleeding in a few minute.

Did you ever see a doctor about it?

Yes Joey, in fact four of them. But they could not find a reason why it bleeds.

Tim, I have a cousin-in-law in the Bronx that has the same problem. His nose bleeds all different times.

Nicky what cousin-in-law does that happens to?

Bruiser you don't know him Joey. He is my wife's third cousin. He told me that he has a twin brother, Salvatore who lives in Italy. Every time there is something going on with Salvatore if he gets hurt in lot of pain,even sometime if Bruiser is upset, nervous his nose starts to bleed, he always tell me that the bleeding has to do with his body chemistry being twins.

Nicky you're making this up? You're blowing smoke up are ass. Then Joey started to laugh.

No, I'm not this is a true story.

Yea I'm going to ask your wife when I see here.

Then Nicky ask me Tim do you have a twin brother? I think so that was what I was told through my life? What do you mean I think so? What you don ta youa know? We been split up since birth I hope to find him one of these days.

See Joey it true. How did I know that Tim had a twin brother!

Lucky guess Nicky, Tim is not sure if he does have a twin brother?

I had been wondering if my brother is in prison or war in Iran or Iraq. I have been getting a lot of these nose bleeds' lately. When I was younger it would hardly happen.

See Joey I know it.

Here they go again Joey and Nicky arguing I was hoping that this interview was ending. I was getting tired, hot and was starting to sweat I could feel the water dropping off my face on to my shirt.

My head was pounding so hard. I was thinking to myself why so many question. I am not applying for a position with the FBI. This is only a freaking garbage company *HELLO.*

Tim do you own a car? Yes sir I'm still making payment on my pickup truck. Nicky voice was making my headache worse. He was so loud as if he was yelling at me from down the hall. His strong Italian accent was hard to understand.

The phone on Joey's desk started to ring excuse me for a minute. I have to grab this call. Joey picked up the phone started talking in Italian. I could not understand him, but I knew that he was getting pissed.

Joey started yelling on phone, his face was red. Within two minutes of Joey's conversation he suddenly slammed the phone down and started to swear.

What's up with the call Joey? Who the hell was that?

We will talk later Nicky, right now let's get through with this interview, and then we will have a meeting.

Then Joey looked at me and said Tim this is what we're going to do, we don't normally hire people without experience. I'm willing to give you a chance we all need to start somewhere.

Thank you, Joey.

Then Nicky stated up with a speech. I'm a going to tell youa up front if you should get into any types of accidents and f— upa my truck I will fire your ass in a heartbeat and the same goes if I catch you stealing from us. Do I makea myselfa clear?

Yes Nicky.

I kept on think to myself what the hell is he talking about stealing? HELLO, what would anyone want to take from a trash company this interview is really bazaar?

Joey is there something you want to say?

Yes, Nicky, Tim I am going to start you off at a lower pay scale. But you can earn extra money working the overtime. After you pass your ninety days probation accidents free, and you're not taking any unnecessary time off. I will bring you up to driver pay scale which is two bucks more an hour then what you are making now. Plus health insurance we provide free for you and your son. Two week's pay vacation after the first year you been here and we have more benefits.

Joey what route is Tim going to drive?

Frankie Route.

What happened to Frankie? Nicky shouted at Joey.

I had to fire that bastard.

When did this happen?

Last week you were on vacation Nicky.

You should have called me on my cell.

No Nicky I was not going to bother you when you are on vacation.

I know how to handle it. Just like your boy. God Bless His Soul Mr. Sinatra would have said.

What's that? Nicky had asked Joey with a puzzling look on his face?

Joey stood up remove his chair, clear his throat, and then smile. He started to sing so loud in that deep Italian voice.

Joey left hand was pretending to hold a microphone. His right hand was pointing out to Nicky, as if he was in the audience watching the show. So You Think You Can Sing. Joey started to sing the song MY WAY.

Joey kept on singing the whole song. Nicky fell to the ground laughing so hard I thought he was going to piss in his pants.

I tried to control myself but I could not help, but to laugh it was so funny. I don't know what is funnier Nicky was on the ground making a fool of him. Or Joey thinking he is such a great singer.

There was a loud knock on the door. Nicky yelled come in as he quickly picked himself up from the floor brushing off this suit pants. Hey Tony comes in.

Dad what are you doing? I heard you from down stair at the front door. Well son what do you say was I good? Yes, dad not bad I forgot that Mr. Sinatra had passed a way I thought he was up here with you.

Then Tony started to laugh. Son this is Tim Ripple he is going to be a driver.

Welcome aboard Tim. Thank You. Tim excused my father is not always crazy like this, just once in a while Ha! ha!

Very funny son.

Dad who's route is Tim doing?

Frankie's route.

Say no more dad. I just heard a rumor about what had happen to Frankie. As I was walking into the driver room to the men's room to drain the main vein. I heard two drivers talking about what had happen.

We will talk about it later son.

Okay I have to run.

Are you done for the day?

No, Dad I only have only two more stopped to go when my truck broke down.

What happen to the truck Nicky asked?

The truck was lifting up the can when two hydraulic hoses on the forks blew. That can was too heavy for that truck to lift.

Son by any chance did you happen to look in the can after you broke down.

Yes Dad the can was filled with big chunks of concrete.

What the f — - they know better Nicky yelled out. They should have called the office and order a large roll-off can for construction debris. Nicky then told Tony leave that freaking can full, do not go back to empty it. I'm going to give the customer the bill for fixing the truck. Those hoses are not cheap? I will take care of this problem Nicky yelled out.

Guys I have to go my truck should be fixed by now. Later guys.

Well Tim I believed we keep you longer than you expected we apologize son.

No problem guys.

Tim you can start this Monday morning at four thirty am the banks have to be picked up by five. You will have two helpers. Butch is a skinny black kid.

Victor, you sure cannot miss him, then Joey start to laugh. Joey had a loud funny laugh. His laugh could make a person laugh. Tim do not wait too long if Butch is not there, give him fifteen minutes only, then you and Victor leave the yard.

I will have someone from the office bring Butch out to you.

Joey you need to talk to Butch to tell him we don't run a freaking taxi service.

Your right Nicky I will.

If he wants this job he needs to come to work on time, like everyone else. Joey, tell him no more drinking on the freaking job.

Do it on his own time not on ours.

Nicky how do you know he is drinking again?

Frankie told me two weeks ago that not only is Butch drinking on the job and he is also smoking pot.

Nicky let's talk about this later.

Tim there is a few things I need to tell you before you leave it will only take few minutes to explain to you.

Okay Joey. Tim I will put the route book in truck 15 on the seat.

The book will tell you what stops to pick up. The customer's name addresses, and how many day a week the stop is to be picked up.

The book will also tell you how big the can is, 6, 8, 10 yard, and how many cans the customer has to dump.

Don't skip any of my customers. If the truck breaks down call me right away. I will notify the customer that you're running late.

If the book said there is one can at a stop and you see two cans don't dump the second can, call me immediately. Go by the book this is your bible.

The stops will be in order if you not sure where these stop are ask the guys they will help you. Any stops that are not in this book don't empty.

Your route starts from down town Hartford to the South End of Hartford into West Hartford then by four o'clock that afternoon you're back in downtown Hartford at the bank once again. Its sounds like it's hard to learn but it's not. The banks are the most important stops they can never be missed.

Tim on your way home down the street there is a big medical building. I need for you to go in and take a drug test.

You're not supposed to start work until your drug test come back with drug free results. It takes about a week to get back.

But I need the work done now and you need to make some money now. I'm going to change the policy please don't tell anyone. Before Joey could say another word Nicky started yelling at him in Italian.

Joey was answering him back in Italian. I could tell by the look in Nicky's face and his tone of voice that whatever Joey was telling me Nicky didn't agree.

Joey, continue talking to me Nicky just sat there and keep quiet.What I was telling you Tim before Nicky interrupted me.

Tim that's enough, go home have a nice weekend, and we will see you Monday. Okay guys I will see you later thank you. I ran to catch the elevator I still can hear Nicky yelling.

Joey what is wrong with Frankie? We treated that boy good.

Your right we did. He did too much drugs and alcohol.

Joey last time his car broke down, didn't you lend him three hundred dollars to get that car fix?

Yes Nicky I did.

Did Frankie ever pay you back?

No, but I will take the money out of his last check this week before I mail the check out to him.

Joey you cannot do that. It is against the law.

Watch me Nicky. I don't give a crap.

I cannot believe you're going to do that.

Chapter Six

Street Smarts

⬥

The weekend is finally here, thank God. I called Duke to see what was happening. We talked for a while; he had filled me in on what was going on. Duke had asked me if I could sell some stocks, and send him out a check for six thousand. It's been four years ago, I began to work on the clubs stock portfolio, with only two thousand dollars. Now, the clubs account had $15,200 in it, between my buying and selling and there quarterly dividends, there account had a profit of over ten thousand dollars in it. Duke told me he and the club were buying another piece of property, right next to their club house. This will be the clubs fourth piece of property on that street.

After my conversation with Duke, I headed out to get Peter from his mother. He was staying over my place for the weekend. We went straight to the Dinosaur State Park in Rocky Hill and took a nice tour around the park. Then we made a dinosaur track out of plaster. It was messy but fun.

Then after lunch, we went to a park to fly a kite. The weather was nice and sunny, and the wind was blowing like crazy which kept the kite up the whole time. It was a perfect day and we had a great weekend together. Sunday afternoon, at five, I brought Peter back to his Mom. I hated having to let him go.

Before I knew it, my alarm was going off, it was 3:00am the time came too fast. I kept hitting the snooze button because I wanted to sleep so bad, knowing I need to get my butt up. I decided on a cold shower that morning instead of a hot one, to wake me up. Got dressed quickly, ran out the door, and headed for seven elevento get some great coffee.

Hello Sue, how's it going?

Good morning Tim, what are you doing here so early?

I'm starting a new job this morning.

What company is it?

Automatic-Waste-Away.

Tim they dump my trash that is a great company. Do you know Joey the owner and his son Tony?

Yes, I just met both of them last Friday in my interview. They seem like nice people.

They are I have been with them going on five years next month. I can't wait that will be my last loan payment. Then I will finally own this store. Joey stops in about four days a week, buys his coffee and bullshits with me all the time. Last year, Joey gave me a present for no special reason and you'll never guess what it was. Two tickets, front row seats, to see the Eagle's in concert at the Hartford Center.

No way. Wow! Sue, that was a nice present.

You got that right it was a great concert. My girlfriend, Karen, owns an Italian bakery on Franklin Ave in Hartford. Joey also has her account. He is always going in her store and buying pastries for his office. A week before Christmas last year, Joey gave her four tickets, front row seats, to see the circus. Karen took her husband and her two kids. They loved the show. Joey is not only a nice man but he sure knows how to run his business and take care of his customers.

Sue, did you ever meet Joey's brother-in-law Nicky?

Ha, Yeah Nicky is a real piece of work.

Well Sue I better go, I don't want to be late on my first day, I will see you soon.

Tim, the coffee is on me have a nice day.

Thank you, Sue.

I pulled into the parking lot, looked at my watch it was 3:50 am. I was getting a little nervous and my palms were sweating. I really didn't know what to expect from the job or the workers. I walked in the side door of the garage and I heard people talking.

Good Morning, you must be Tim Ripple.

Yes sir, I am. Good morning.

My name is Jim Piper, I'm the head mechanic.

It's nice to meet you.

Nicky told me to give you this list and to go over it with you. Let's take a walk. I will show you your truck.

That sounds good Jim.

Tim I do this all the time to all new drivers, it's not just you. Nicky is fussy with these trucks.

I hear you Jim.

Every morning you will check out your truck oil, windshield fluid, lights, horn, the air in the tires, signal lights, and your fuel before you leave the yard. If there is any problem with this truck let me know before you leave. I'm here early every morning. I can fix it or switch your truck out with a spare truck. Make sure you finish your route early afternoon on Fridays. Give yourself plenty of time. Nicky made all the routes lighter on Friday so the drivers and their helpers can wash their trucks. He likes the trucks cleaned inside and out, and believe me. That man will come in on Saturday morning and check out all the trucks. He knows who did and didn't do it. When Monday morning comes around, Nicky will call the drivers of a dirty truck and have them stop in his office before they could head home and chew them out. When its time for their yearly review, He will tell the drivers the date, time, even the weather, and how many times in one year that driver was called in his office for a dirty truck, he's like an elephant, he never forgets, and he will cut your raise down. Let's say you were getting one dollar more an hour because that's the going rate with a perfect record for the year, well Nicky will cut down that raise to thirty five cents an hour. That's when you start seeing a big turn over with drivers and helpers. Nicky is so cheap he squeaks. So words of advice, wash your truck every Friday. And bring the truck into the garage empty at night. Trust me heads will roll if the truck is not empty.

No riders in your truck except your helpers. Some of the guys were taking their girlfriends on the route with them. Nicky found out what was going on, and fired those drivers. I still can't figure out why any driver would want to take their girlfriends in their trucks. It's crazy, there are much nicer places to knock off a piece of ass than in a garbage truck. Then he started laughing.

Also, here is a phone for you, in case Nicky or Joey needs to get a hold of you. Keep the phone on at all times with the volume up. Park the truck in your parking spot only, they are all numbered. Keep the keys in the ignition when you park the truck at night, in case of an emergency and we have to move the trucks. There was a fire at the old garage two years ago, the drivers didn't leave the keys in the truck and Joey lost three new trucks. All three drivers were let go the next day. I won't ever forget that day; Joey and Nicky were going crazy. Tim, do you have any questions?

No, I'm good Jim, thank you.

Here is your route book, once you learn these stops the job is a piece of cake. Let me explain how this route book works. Your first stop is the bank on the corner of Main and Pearl Street downtown Hartford. This stop is pickup five days a week, Monday through Friday, twice a day. The bank is your first and last stop of the day and needs to be picked up after four o'clock that afternoon. All the cars that are parked down in the alley will be out of there by four o'clock. The bank closes at three. Also, Pizza Plus is Tuesdays and Fridays twice a week. If you have any questions ask your helpers. They know the stops well and will help you out. Your helpers knows the city well, and they can show you ways to cut down travel time when needed. Your truck number is 60.

Jim walked me over to the truck, Wow it is nice.

This truck isn't even a year old and only has 2000 miles, go ahead and jump in.

The truck was sweet, and I could smell the leather seats. It had an automatic transmission which was nice. It also had a AM/FM radio, CD player, blue tooth that connect automatic to your smart phone to play your own music. It has two, Bose's speakers in each door. With power steering and power windows. It had self-defrosting windows, air conditioning, three different outlets for chargers. A sunroof window to let fresh air in. I didn't expect so much inside a garbage truck. It is unbelievable.

Oh one more thing Tim, before Jim could finish his sentence, a loud voice yelled out.

Good morning, are we having a meeting here?

No, I'm just showing Tim the truck.

Tim this is Butch. Jim introduced us to each other.

It's Nice to meet you Butch.

Right back at you.

That Dude that's running over here now is Victor. Jim said to me, and then he introduced us to one another. Victor this is Tim he will be your new driver.

It's nice to meet you Tim.

Jim, what happened to Frankie? Butch asked.

Joey had to let him go.

Why what did Frankie do?

I don't know Butch, Joey never told me, it's really none of my business, I never asked.

That really sucks Butch replied.

I could tell by their conversation that I was in for a rough day. It seems that Butch was close to Frankie. Victor didn't say anything. He just looked and listened to Jim and Butch. Now I know why Joey was laughing when he mentioned Victor. Victor is a big dude. He was about 6 feet, 5 inches tall, around 180 lbs Spanish light skinned, and built with all muscle, and no fat. Victor's neck and arms were covered with beautiful detailed tattoos, real nice art work.

You could tell Victor spent an arm and a leg on the tattoos, no pun intended?!Ha ha! Victor had a bald head, a big nose that was flattened, and a gold earring in his left ear, with a resemblance to that man on the detergent bottles. I would say Victor was in his late twenty's early thirty's. He was dressed neat even his jeans were pressed.

Butch is about 5 feet 9 inches, black skinned, looked to be in his early twenties and about 130 lbs. He was a skinny guy, he looked under nourished. He was dressed sloppy, the jeans he had on were dirty with stains. He smelled like whiskey, it is bad. When he spoke, you could see that his teeth were rotted and he smelled like he hadn't showered in weeks.

Well guys, I have to go.

Okay, thank you Jim.

Anytime bud.

Tim, good luck and have a nice day.

Hey Victor, I didn't have a chance to finish checking out the truck yet.

No problem Tim.

Victor started to yell at Butch. Check all the lights and tires, I will show Tim how to check the engine oil and the rest of the truck.

Okay bro, I got you covered Victor. Butch yelled back at him.

I drove out of the yard and Victor gave me directions to the first stop the bank. I pulled up and could not believe how small, narrow and steep the alley was. There just didn't seem like there was enough room for the truck to make it in.

Yo man, you can do it Tim, Line up the front of the truck with the driveway across the street, watch out for people walking behind the truck, and check your side mirrors all the time when you're backing up. Can you see the fire hydrant on the edge of the sidewalk in your right side mirror?

Yea Victor, I see it.

Watch out for it, don't hit it.

Okay, here's the scoop Dude. Victor started to yell. You only have a foot on each side of the truck from the walls, so back the truck straight down into the alley and don't turn the wheel until you have the truck half way down the alley. If you should turn the truck to much either side you will clip those big mirrors and dent the door.

Butch and I have seen two drivers this year get fired for smashing fenders, mirrors, and doors steps, all from this freaking stop here. When we didn't get along with a driver, we would walk away when the drivers was trying to back down the alley. We would both just laugh and watch them smash the truck. I don't think I have to tell you what happened next.

Yes Victor I got your drift.

Now as you back down the alley, it will get wider then there is no problem. Can you see the big yellow line on the ground.

Yes I do.

Put the back of the truck on that line don't back down any further.

I got you Victor.

Yo,Tim.

What's up Butch.

Just remember your helpers can make or break you. Ha! ha! Right, Victor?

Right on Bro.

I was backing up trying to get down the alley and I was getting pissed; it took me four tries to get the truck in right. Boy it was tight.

I could hear Butch yell.

Yo, Bro you made it.

Then Victor yelled out Hey Tim great job

Thanks guys for guiding me.

Hey, Tim catch Butch threw a bat towards me.

What's up with this?

Hang on to it, you might need it.

What for?

Rats Bro! Ha! ha!

Tim besides dumping the can, we need to pick up all the boxes on the ground, sometimes the rats sleep under them boy they get pissed when you wake them up. They will run after you try to corner you and attack you. The rats hurt too, especially when they get their teeth in you. Butch knows, he's been bitten twice.

Yea you got that right Victor, I sure did.

So Tim, take the bat and whack them hard. Get them before they get you Bro.

Tim, help me roll out the six yard can to the truck.

Okay.

Let me show you how to dump this can. There is a certain technique.

Sure Victor.

Line the end of the can up to the two ends of the truck evenly. You will see that on each end of the truck there are cut grooves where the handle on the can goes into the truck, and then put the hook which is connected to the winch, in the middle of the back of the can, where you will see the round piece of metal. Hook the can and then push the blue handle down that will pick the can up and dump it. If you hold the handle down too long, the winch will pull the can right into the hopper. It's a pain in the ass trying to get the can out of the truck. So with your left hand holding the can, guide it so it does not fall in. At the same time, push the blue handle back with your right hand so it will go back to the ground. Then take the winch off and roll the can back where it came from. It's that easy Dude.

I got you Victor.

Tim, bring the red handle to you. That will bring the blade toward you to scooping the trash up and compressing the garbage automatic. When the truck is full the blades well not crush any more garbage. Oh and by the way, watch your fingers the blade will cut them off. I saw this happen last year to that driver named Pat. That boy lost his left hand. It was so gross blood was all over the freaking place. I was puking my guts out. Butch do you remember?

Yea, barely, I had passed out when I saw his bloody fingers on the ground.

So Butch, whatever happen to this guy Pat?

He is still around? Yes Tim with no left hand.

Yo Victor the boys must be paying Pat big bucks.

The last that I heard Mark was trying to sue both Nicky and Joey.

They both went to court last month, but I don't know what had happen to his case.

I never heard any more about it, it's been hush-hush.

That's why you see that big sign on the back of the trucks telling you to keep your hands away from the blade.

Thanks Victor I will watch my hands.

Butch, are you through yet?

I just killed two rats.

Yo Butch, remove that dead rat you hit off the walkway, you know the bank will call Joey in a heartbeat if they see them. H E L L O.

Okay.

Victor, everything is picked up.

Let's get out of here.

We headed towards the next stop, when Victor said Tim you seem like a clean cut kid, what the hell are you doing here?

I just went through a bad divorce, and needed to change my life, so I decided switching my career. I'm also going to finish my education and get my degree in law. I have one year left of law school. Then I'm planning to open up my own law firm in criminal and family law.

You won't catch me going back to school. Butch said with a snicker.

Then Victor asked why Butch why you'd rather be working in the back of this garbage truck the rest of your life?

No way dude, I have made a lot more money by dealing.

Butch the cops will catch your skinny black ass and will throw you in the slammer. Then you're sorry ass will be calling, Tim up to represent you. Ha! ha!

You're very funny Victor.

Butch shut up. Let Tim talk.

Hey Tim, take a right the second house on the left is Joey's doctor. They will call our office if we are running late, or when we try to skip there pick up. They're a pain in the ass. Back the truck up to the side door on the right side of the office and just watch out for the fence, it's easy to hit.

Tim stay here in the truck, Butch and I will get this one. You can check out the book to see what stop we're going to after we come back from the dump. The truck will be full after this can.

Ok you got it Victor.

I sat in the truck and watched both of them in the mirror. I could see Victor's hands going in every direction as he was yelling at Butch. He was yelling right back at Victor, pointing fingers at the ground. I could not hear what they were talking about the truck was too loud to roll the windows down. When they got back into the truck, I could tell by their faces, they were mad about something.

Tim take a right, lets head for the dump. I followed Victor's directions to the next location.

Stop in front of the scale Then drive slowly on to the scale you don't want to break it, a lady in the scale house will wave at you to go, once she records the weight of the truck. Then drive off the scale slowly.

Ok Victor thanks.

Tim do you see the sign on the left side?

The sign read Household Garbage Up The Hill.

Got it.

Tim that hill is steep and a bitch when it's snowing or sleet it's slippery.

Damn, that smell is gross.

Hey Victor, tell Tim about the dead body you found.

Butch, get your black ass out of the truck and unlock those latches, and for the third time, don't slam the freaking door or I will make you part of it.

Tim, put the PTO on so we can dump the truck.

You got it Victor.

So Victor, you found a dead body?

Yea, last year I was watching this driver dumping out his truck and all of a sudden a bunch of birds and seagulls started to attack this plastic bag, it was crazy, like a scene from a movie. Normally they don't go for plastic, there's so much garbage that the birds can pick and choose what to feast on. Then Butch yelled at me to move that freaking truck, you're holding up the line.

Just when I put the truck into first gear, I looked back in the mirror and saw a bird pulling something out of the plastic bag, it was a human arm. I jammed on my breaks and jumped out of the truck to talk to homeboy Pat is a city worker at the dump. He was checking out the loads from different trucks dumping the trash. I was able to get his attention I showed him the seagull on the ground with the human arm in its mouth.

Homeboy had stopped the driver from leaving, the driver was pissed. Then he started yelling at homeboy telling him he didn't want to stick around for the cops he was running late on his route already. Homeboy walked over where the driver had just dumped the trash. Then he started kicking the garbage around, and ended up kicking a human head that was unattached to the body. Then he called the police. We could not stick around any longer we were running late that day. We had a truck break down early that morning, and Joey was ripping, we were already two hours behind schedule.

So what happened, Victor?

The body was of a white female in her late twenties. The newspaper said she was raped then murder. The killer removed her head and left arm from her body. They never caught the killer.

Man that sucks.

Tim, slow down Ha! ha! Butch is scared of heights.

Hey Tim pull the truck over now.

Butch we are in the middle of the freaking hill, and I have traffic right behind us. Why?

The bumps are killing me. I have to drain the main vein.

Can't you wait until we get to the bottom?

Nope.

So we stopped to let Butch out.

Hey Tim, look at that those guys over there.

What are they putting up?

It looks like a huge sign.

Tim what does the sign say, I can't read it from here.

The sign says 1-Only one person out of the truck must wear safety vest. 2-No talking on cell phone or texting in any part in dump. 3-Use only public restrooms. 4-No smoking anywhere in this landfill.

We both laughed, and then Victor rolled down the window started yelling out. Hey Butch put your wiener back in your pants. Get your ass in this truck now.

Butch walked back over, to the truck zipping his pants up. Man that felt good.

Butch read the new sign. Ha! ha!

What new sign?

That's the one on your left side.

You got to be kidding me.

No Butch I don't think they're kidding Victor said laughing so hard.

Yo Victor do you know that dude they call Bean?

Yea, he's going out with my niece Jean.

Well I was talking to him last night at the club on the avenue. The dude was telling me that one of the city workers, big bad Terry Adams, who was operating one of those big bull dozers at the landfill and he didn't see the ground man, Ricky Tops.

Ricky was on the cell phone texting instead of looking around directing the trucks in and out for dumping. That boy was run over by the dozer, and flattened like a pancake.

Wow, are you serious?

Yea Dude.

What happened to Terry? I asked Butch.

He is charged with first degree murder.

Who is pressing charges?

Ricky's old lady. She is also suing the city.

My boy Slim Jim told me that Terry never checked out the dozer that morning. He just ran it. The backup alarm was not working. That dozer should have been out of service. He is in jail waiting for his trial. He does not have the money for bail that sucks.

Dude, that's what the boy gets. I personally believed its Terry the operators fault. Never use any equipment that's not running right, dead lock that bitch. He could have grabbed another dozer from their garage that was working right. Safety comes first. You can't put a price on safety Butch. That's probably why that new sign is up for insurance purposes. The city is going to cover their ass for now on.

Chapter Seven

Fight for What is Right

The next morning I caught up with Victor while leaving the yard.

Victor, if you don't mind me asking.

Go ahead Dude speak your mind, I'm all ears.

Why are you working here?

You should be working at a gym or be a bodyguard in Hollywood.

I wish I could Tim, it's not that easy. I owe Joey my life.

What do you mean?

I was a heavy weight boxer.

Wow, you were?

You mean to tell me you've never heard of me or seen me on the news or in the ring? Tim, my ring name was Slugger. To this day people I bump into still call me Slugger. Victor, I'm sorry, but I have never followed boxing. I could tell I hit a nerve and Victor is pissed.

Man, I can't believe that you've never seen me fight. I've been on TV, in newspapers, magazines even on the internet.

I've fought at many different places, casinos and civic centers around the country. The money was great; I was able to buy Mom a beautiful home in West Hartford. I paid cash for it. I was so happy to get Mom out of the ghetto. Being the champion was a fast life, money, women, drugs, and cars, anything I wanted. I won the undefeated title. Man what a great feeling it was to be a champ, but my world was coming to an end for me. The Boxing Association took my title away from me.

Why is that?

Well, Tim, to make a long story short. Danny the opponent was a great friend of mind. We grew up in the projects together, went to the same schools with the same classes, so we both go way back. His son, Danny Jr, is my godson. Danny had put up a good fight that night. He was kicking my ass in the third round. I had hit the ground hard, my nose was broken in two parts and I was bleeding like crazy. My left eye was black and blue.

Tim head for the fish market on Park Street.

Man I hate that stop.

I have to agree with you Butch it sucks.

So Victor, continue what happened?

Well, I wouldn't give up I got up and started fighting back. I thought it was over, I was bleeding so badly, and I could not see all that well. Everything was blurred and to top that off I was losing my strength.

I threw my last punch hit Danny on the right side of his face. He went down hit the ground hard and never got back up. I really didn't hit him that hard. It was like a tap. I was so exhausted.

It was a good feeling to win that title, but it concerned me that Danny was knocked out. Within minutes, the ambulance came and took him away. Three days later, Danny passed away in the hospital. Doctor was able to do an MRI while Danny was still alive and they had found a large tumor next to his brain. By the size of the tumor doctor said it was about a year old.

Tim, take a left into this parking lot. Let's do this stop at the bus company. Joey just got this account last week.

Butch grab that eight yarder and all those boxes on the ground, I will back the truck up to it.

Be very careful. This place is so busy these buses are flying through this yard. They don't even follow their own eight mile an hour speed limit.

Butch, I'm going to take Tim with me we will grab the other two cans on the top of the hill, see you in little while.

Okay Bro.

So Victor, what happened next?

Gail, Danny's wife called and asked me if I knew anything about his tumor. I told her no, and that Danny had never said anything to me about it. If I had known I would have talked him out of the fight. We always looked out after each other.

So you think Danny knew about the tumor?

Yes, I believe so, and he never said anything about it to any of us.

Gail had signed the paper work which gave permission for the hospital doctor to get Danny's medical records to find out what Danny's doctor was hiding. It was a coincidence the next day Gail had received a call from Dr. Harris, Danny's doctor not knowing that Danny was dead. The Doctor told Gail he had schedule Danny's surgery to remove the tumor next Wednesday at 7:00 am at the surgery center on Jefferson Street. Gail told me she lost it; she started yelling at the doctor Harris, then hung-up on him.

Next, she called Tom, Danny's coach and asked him if he know about the tumor. He told Gail they all knew about the tumor. Danny said this was his last fight before he went in for surgery. Gail told Tom that he and Doctor Harris should have stopped Danny from fighting.

They should have canceled the fight. Then she hung up on Coach Tom. Then she called me up right after and was just crying on the phone.

Victor it doesn't make sense. Why didn't the doctor stop the fight?

He was getting a big kick back of cash from the coach Tom. Whether Danny wins or loses the fight he still gets paid big bucks, but if the fight is canceled no one's make any money. So, Doctor Harris had signed the physical papers saying that Danny was in good health and was ready to fight.

I got you now Victor, Those greedy bastards.

Man you got that right.

After I got off the phone with Gail, I was pissed. I was not in the right frame of mind. I should have never gone over to coach Jerry's home but I wanted to talk to him.

As we talked the conversation was getting hot. Coach Tom was trying to cover everything up. He was getting mad and pushed me telling me to leave. So I shoved him back. Coach Tom had tripped on a pair of shoes that was on the floor near the front door.

He fell on one of the tables in the hallway and hit his head hard on the floor, and passed out. The Coach's wife heard the noise and she ran into the hallway to see what was going on. She screamed and grabbed a vase of fresh flowers that was on the table then threw them at me. I ducked quickly and the vase went over my head and right through the front glass door behind me. Glass shattered everywhere.

Then she called the police on me and an ambulance for Coach Tom. I was scared, so I ran to my car and was ready to split when the cops blocked me in. They grabbed and cuffed me and threw me into the back of their car then I heard the ambulance driver telling the cops on the radio that Coach Tom was pronounced dead. Tim I will tell you the rest of my story later just remind me.

ok Victor

Hey can you help me drag this can to the truck it's got a broken wheel. I had asked Victor. I pulled from the front and he pushed from the back of the can, and we got both cans to the truck.

I got to tell Joey about the bad wheels so we can get it fixed. Let's get Butch and head into the yard, it's getting late.

That night, I called Peter to see how he was doing. He was so happy he was going to start baseball tomorrow after school. Then I told him I would pick him up soon.

It's been a few weeks now and I seem to be doing well with my new job. It sounds crazy but I really enjoy it.

A few weeks had gone by we just got done picking up at LaSalle Giant Grinders. Victor was yelling telling me the next stop was at the apartments on Retreat Street. Do you remember how to get there?

Yea, let's do it.

As we pulled into the parking lot Victor started talking. This is how the game works we will take turns. We all have our own can. Lift the can slowly, be careful, the rats will get pissed and will start to jump out. Stand back they will attack you in a heartbeat. Hey Butch, shut the radio off back here. It's got to be quiet we don't want to startle the rats just yet.

I got it.

Whoever hits a rat the farthest distance wins? And the two losers will buy the winner a case of beer. Are you ready? Butch go for it Tim lift the can slowly.

I had never seen anything like it before. There were so many rats. They came flying and jumping out of the big can.

Watch out Butch, There is two rats coming toward you. {Thwack} All you do is just keep on swinging that bat fast until the can is dump and the rats are gone.

Nice hit Butch.

Ready Victor go for it, wow you really hit that rat far. I think you have me beat. Butch yelled out.

Tim, it's your turn you're up.

Victor stopped the can and we watched all the rats start racing out.{Thwack!} One rat went flying in the air. {Thwack!} Keep swinging Tim, you're missing them.

Lift the can higher I yelled out.

There you go, you got it. {Thwack!} {Thwack!}

There had to be around fifteen rats at the same time, jumping out of the 8yard can. Then all of sudden we heard a loud scream that came from across the parking lot.

It sounded like an old lady yelling. Help! Help! There's a bloody rat that just flew on my lap. Who the hell did this to me? She kept on screaming, people came out of their houses to see what was going on.

Great shot, Tim. You hit that rat all the way over there.

The lady was sitting in her rocking chair on her porch reading the paper when the rat hit the paper and fell on to her lap. Then we heard, what the hell are you boys doing? She screamed.

Let's get the hell out of here I shouted. Within an hour my cell phone was ringing. Oh shit, it's Joey you better answer it Tim.

Hey, Joey.

Tim, what the hell are you guys doing? I just got a freaking call from the police. Which one of you guys hit that rat that landed on the lady's lap?

I did sir.

I need to see you in my office when you finish the route today.

Yes Sir.

There is a memo in the driver's room that has been hanging on the board for about a year now. It's about hitting rats. I guess you guys don't read the board everyday like you are supposed to. I will see you later.

Yo Tim, What the hell did Joey say Butch asked me?

What didn't he say? That man is pissed he wants to see me when we come in his office.

Tim, tell Joey we could not help it, there are too many rats here and they are going to attack us.

Joey was going to send an exterminator over here to get rid of these damn rats last year, but he never did. Tim that memo was up on the board way before you started here. Let's go to the dump, we cannot get any more in this truck.

Joey also mentioned he wants us to pick up the banks this afternoon.

Damn it, what's wrong with big bad Mackie Brown? You know that bitch is a lazy ass. I'm getting tired of doing that boy's work.

Me too, Victor agreed with Butch.

Yo Victor, is it okay if Tim drops me off on Main Street, while you and Tim go to the dump? I will stay here at the bank and make sure there are no cars blocking the cans.

Butch, Do you have your phone? Is your phone bill paid for this month? Then Victor started laughing.

Very funny Victor.

Thanks I thought it was too.

Butch, don't do anything stupid. No dope or booze.

Don't worry, Victor I won't. See you guys later.

Please don't slam the freaking door. Damn that boy never listens to me. Victor yelled and Butch slammed the door.

As I started up the hill at the dump Victor yelled out.

Tim, that guy is pointing to the left pile to dump. Okay Victor, I'm going to jump out and unlock the back. Okay ready. Tim let me drive to the bank if you don't mind.

No I don't mind go for it.

Man I hate this hill. Hang on.

Watch out for that slow poke in front of us.

That's Billy Green {Honk Honk}. Hey, Billy you need to retire your old ass boy. Then he started to laugh.

Hey Slugger, how the hell are you son?

Good, I got to pass you or I will be part of this truck coming up the hill, later bud. Wow that was a close one.

Tim call Butch, tell him we will be there shortly.

But Victor we still got twenty minutes before we are at the bank.

Tim it will take Butch twenty minutes to get to the bank from where ever he is at now. I know how that boy works. He is never on time.

I got you. So Victor, tell me what happen after the police took you away?

Well to make another long story short, I was arrested for first-degree murder. I got twenty years in the slammer at Enfield prison. I was lucky I only did eight years, thanks to Joey. It's funny how thing work out in life they stood by me at my trial, I even used Joey's attorney, David Jackson and he is great. Mom worked for Joey. She cleaned his office and his house, cooked and babysat for him.

Oh wow.

She would always brag about me to Joey; she was so proud of me. One day Mom gave tickets to Joey and Tony to see me fight at the casino. I was in my dressing room getting ready. I heard a knock on the door. Mom had brought Joey and Tony in and introduced them to me since then we all three became good friends. Tony was young and shy he was always polite, he didn't say much when he was with the old man Joey. But he would always talk my ear off when Joey wasn't around. There is about six years between us. I was like Tony's older brother. Tony would follow me at different fights; he would bring his girlfriends or the chums he hung out with, and introduce them to me. He was proud of me.

Joey tried hard to get me out of the slammer early. Joey had a meeting with the State and the warden. He came up with a program he would hire ex-cons, welders, painters, helpers, and drivers. But if the cons screw up in any way he will go back to prison and finish out their sentence. Joey asked for me along with four other inmates. The four guys were no problem and they were released fast.

It was me the warden didn't like. He told Joey that if I was ever sent back for any reason, I will have to start my sentences again all over from day one.

Fifteen years with no early release. I had to sign a document with that in writing to be released. Joey looked good, he was on TV, newspapers and other states followed his work program. Not only did this move help out his businesses, but it also help out his bank account. Every ex-con he hired the state is sending Joey a check for 150.00 a week for each ex-con that stays working for him.

Dam Victor, Joey is smart.

You got that right Tim.

Okay Tim, Butch both of you guys watch out for me when I back down this alley.

Butch what's up?

Not much Tim I just kicked out two bums that were sleeping in the boxes.

I came down when a lady got out of her car she parked right in front of the can. So I ask her to move she was cool. Tim hook up the can and dump it. Hey Butch help me grab those boxed.

Let's get out of here.

Yo Tim you can drive?

Oh Victor.

Take a right this is Park Street. We are going to the fish market you will see a yellow building on the right.

Drive in the back parking lot, and backup to the dock where those two cans and boxes on the ground.

You got it Victor.

Yo Tim be careful watch out for captain hook. He is known to hook a few people in his time. ThenVictor keeping on laughing.

Butch is not kidding the Dude that works there has a hook on his right hand, and a black patch covering his left eye?

What happen to him I had asked?

No one seems to know Victor replied.

As we all got out of the truck I followed Victor. Butch had disappeared on us. Victor and I were cleaning the dock off, Picking up the empty smelly fish boxes.

I turn around and noticed Butch, walking next doors and was talking to a man in front of the Chinese restaurant, The Red Dragon.

Then, Butch started walking over to us with empty boxes, with Chinese writing on them, throwing them into the truck.

Hey, Butch are you going to help us out?

Yea dog you know that.

But, you had disappeared on us Dude.

Hey, man what's up with that?

What are you talking about Tim?

I'm talking about you leaving us all the work, while your bullshitting with that man over there.

Dude I just got us all some lunch. Three orders of egg rolls, pork fried rice, boneless spare ribs the lunch special.

Are you hungry Tim?

Yes I am but there is one problem.

What's the problem Tim?

That Red Dragon Restaurant is not in the route book, I checked.

Yo, Bro this is one of our benefits of the job.

Yo, Man that's one of our stops.

Right, Victor.

Right on Butch.

We have a lot more.

Let's see we have a liquor store, meat market we get nice tasty steaks every Thursdays night after work.

We also have a Barber shop that cuts our hair and he gives us a free shave. We have pizza restaurant twice a week we eat for free, plus we have a video store we get free movies. Tim the list goes on. We even have a veterinarian that gives us free dog food. We are talking the best expensive food and we get all shots for our dogs. Dude you can't beat that.

Yes you can, by stop stealing.

Yo Bro we got it made we are going to include you in all of our stops.

Guys I'm not getting involved stealing from Joey or anyone else for that matter.

Yo Bro, are you afraid? Don't worry we will not get caught.

That's what they all say Butch. But down the road they all get caught, but go ahead enjoy your food boys.

Yo where are you going?

I'm going to get me a sausage grinder. I walked across the street to Sally's Giant Grinder.

After lunch I jumped in the truck, turned down the loud rap music that they were playing. They both looked at me but never said a word.

The rest of the day was so quiet both of them were not talking to me, I could tell they were both were mad at me. Thank God, the day is over.

That night I went to school to sign up for a course in criminal law. To my surprise the school is offering two new credited courses DNA 101, Body Language 101.

I was always hoping that someday they would teach this course D N A my dream came true. It has been twenty minute that I have been standing waited in line at the book store.

I was reading the schools new paper there was an article welcoming Professor Ron James to the school. Prof. James is a retired police captain from, New Orleans. He has two doctors degree, one degree in criminal law and the second degree is in immigration. He was an attorney for twelve years then served as a Judge for six years.

He decided to leave New Orleans and came to Connecticut to be with his daughter and three grandkids.

Prof. James wife was killed in a train crash two years ago. I had picked up my head to stretch my neck that is killing me, when I noticed a middle age man in a suit walked passed by me.

Excused me Sir, I yelled out. He heard me and then he stopped turned around to see where the voice came from. I waved at him to get his attention; everyone in line had stopped talking and just kept on staring at us.

Are you Professor James?

Yes I am?

I'm Tim Ripple nice to meet you.

Same, here Tim.

I just sign up for two of your courses.

That's great.

I'm teaching four courses this semester.

Which two did you sign up for?

DNA 101, Body Language 101

Good choices.

I'm really looking forward to teach at this school.

Tim it's has been nice to meet you.

Same here.

Tim I have to go, I'm running late I have a faculty meeting.

I will see you next week in class, ok have a nice evening.

You do the same.

After waiting one hour in line, I finally got my books and headed home, I was beat.

CHAPTER EIGHT

WHEN IT RAINS IT POURS

G ood morning guys.

Good morning Dude.

Tim, did you check out the truck? Yes Victor.

It's time to roll. Let's get the hell out of here, head for the bank.

You got it Victor.

Hey, Tim drop me off at the corner on Main and State Street. I will go and get us some coffee.

Okay,Victor you got it.

I will meet you and Butch at the bank

Tim, how do you like your coffee? Light with cream,one sugar.

Yo Butch, I like my coffee black, just like the way I like my ladies.

Got Yo Bro chow. Okay I will see you later.

Finally I got my seat back Butch said to me.

Don't get too comfortable Butch, You need to get your ass outside and guide me back down into that alley.

Dude it so cold out there. I'm freezing my ass off now and I'm still sitting here in the truck with the heat blasting.

Can't you see it's nasty out there Tim?

Yes, Butch I see.

Tim the sleet is coming down faster and bigger it seem like there is no end to it.

I didn't say a word I just looked at him.

Then he jumped out of the truck. He was pissed slammed the door hard, the mirror from the door had moved, I jumped out of the truck to adjust it. As I was backing up, I could not see Butch in either mirror. I stopped the truck, jumped out and started yelling, Butch, where the hell are you?

I'm down here Tim.

Get up here and guide me please.

Hold on.

I could smell the burning pot in the air Butch was down in the alley getting high. I ran back to the truck, jumped in and started to back up. Butch still never came up to help me out. As I was backing up I felt the truck slipping and sliding on the ice to the right side.

All sudden I heard Victor voice yelling Tim stop the truck stop now.

It was too late. I felt the truck jerk and heard a loud noise, like I just hit something. Sure enough water was shooting all over the truck. I quickly stopped the truck, jumped out and ran to the back of the truck to see what I had hit.

I was getting wet and I was freezing fast my jacket was all ice. It was twenty degrees out at 5:00 am in the morning. To my surprised I just hit the fire hydrant on the right side of the truck, knocked it down flashed to the side walk. Nonstop water was shooting up so high in the air that when the water came down it turns into ice instantly the street and sidewalk is one thick piece of ice. What a mess.

Finally Butch came up from the alley.

Butch, stop those car now have them back up to Main Street. They will never make it going down that street. They won't be able to stop when they reach the end of Pearl Street. They will drive right through the intersection and could hit a bus or people or a car crossing the intersection.

Yo, what shall I tell the people that want to drive down?

Dude, just give them a bullshit story. You're good at that. Ha! ha!

Very funny Victor.

Tell them there is a fire at the coffee shop or, a bum got shot on the street. I don't care what you say make up something.

Victor, I thought all fire hydrants were drain and shut off during the winter months so the pipes wont freeze and damage the road.

Yes Tim your right they all have to drain and shut off. Then in the spring the City paints then and turn them on if the kids don't get there before them.

Someone screwed up big time with this fire hydrant.

I'm so nervous Victor. I can still remember hearing that loud voice and mean look of Nicky's, and his famous words he said.

If you should fukin—up my truck, you are fired. I think Joey will be ok with it! But what will Nicky say or do.

Tim you need to call Joey now. It's better if you call him, than for him to call you finding out, especially from a cop. He has to know what's going on. Go ahead Tim call Joey.

Okay, Victor I will.

As I tried to dial the phone my hands were shaken so bad. Yo, Tim gave me the phone I will dial his number for you.

Thanks Victor

It's ringing take the phone Tim.

Hey, Joey

What up Tim? It's early for you to be calling me. What is wrong? What happen?

Well, Joey. I just had an accident on Pearl Street. I knocked over a fire hydrant. The water was never turned off its still shooting out and it won't stop.

Tim, what the f—- did you just say?

I've have knock over a fire hydrant I shouted out.

Get the hell out of there now and head over to West Hartford now.

Do the route backwards.

But Joey, leaving the scene of an accident I will get screwed if I get caught. I might end up doing time. If anyone gets hurts or killed trying to go down this icy road!

Did anyone see you hit the fire hydrant?

Yes, two cars were trying to come down the street they got stuck on the ice. We were able to get them out of here.

How bad did you f−k up my truck?

Will the back step is mangle and crushed.

Tim leave there now I will cover you I promise.

I will catch up to you later.

Ok Joey see you later bye.

Tim, where the hell was Butch?

Victor that boy was down there in the bottom of the alley getting high.

Hey Butch what happened?

Get in the truck now let's get out of here.

I put the truck in drive then I hit the gas. The tires kept on spinning on the ice.

The right side of the truck was covered with ice from the water shooting out from the hydrant.

Yo, Tim we are stuck.

No way.

Tim drop the shift into first gear, Hit the gas slow, then put the truck in reverse rock the truck slowly.

Okay, Victor the truck started to go. You can't go down the street. We will get stuck its all ice.

Yo, Tim this is one way go up the street, you're going the wrong way.

Victor I have no choice. Let's hope no cars are coming down. We will be screwed.

Tim your phone is ringing again.

Tim, can you hear me? H E L L O.

Yes, Joey.

Are you out of there yet?

I just heard on the radio scanner that the fire trucks and the police are heading over there… get the hell out of there now.

Boy, I would have say at this time now Joey's blood pressure must be boiling by now.

Yo thanks to you Butch, you freaking dickhead.

If you weren't so busy getting freaking high this would not had happen. You should have been there guiding Tim into the alley. What the hell is wrong with you Butch?

I was going to.

You're so full of crap Butch. I jumped out of the truck calling you to help me out and you were ignoring me.

Tim, Bang a right on to Park Street… now quickly.

Ok Victor.

Oh, crap what's wrong Tim? There is a cop on my ass with his lights flashing and siren is on. I'm pulling over let's see what he wants. I'm hoping no one saw me hit the fire hydrant.

Good Morning, I need to see your license and registration please. I hope you have a C D L license and endorsement on it to drive this truck young man.

Yes officer I do.

Here you are Sir.

Thank you.

The officer kept on steering at Victor checking out his tattoos' and is sniffing the air in the truck as if he doing a line of coke.

I smell pot in this truck.

Who's the one that was smoking the weed?

Do you want me to get a search warrant?

No sir.

Then Butch said to the cop it was a bad smelling stale cigar. I had just lit it I started to smoke it then I was choking so bad that I had just toasted that crappy cigar out the window as Tim was turning the corner.

It better had been a cigar.

I will be back

Then the cop walked over to his car and was talking on the microphone as he was writing something down.

Butch how much pot do you have on you Victor asked him?

None I had smoked the last joint at the bank.

Dude, don't piss on my back and tell me it raining out. You get my drift.

Yo Dude I'm not bullshitting you Victor.

Dude right now this would not be happening to us if you did your freaking job.

Yo I was Victor.

You're lying to me Dude.

Don't say another freak in word. You messed us up. Don't try to get out of it Butch. Dude, don't go there shut up. I'm losing my patience with you bitch. If you keep it up, I will throw your ass out of this truck after I beat the crap out of you. Do you get my drift? Boy I'm not playing Victor screamed at Butch.

Butch shut up quickly knew Victor he was pissed.

Victor I'm screwed.

Tim don't worry Joey has connection he will get you off.

Tim wipes off the sweat off your face your dripping bad.

Here comes the cop now.

Here you are son then the cop handed me a ticket. I stopped you because your left front signal light is out.

Did you check out your truck this morning before leaving?

Yes sir I did.

All the light was working. That bulb must of just have gone out now.

You need to get the light fix. I'm giving you a written warning, you have twenty four hours. If you get stopped again for the same light out after twenty four hours you as the driver will get fined one hundred fifty dollars and two points on you license.

Officer there is an auto parts store down the street I will stop in and get a bulb and fix the light now.

Okay young man be careful have a nice day.

My phone started ringing.

Tim put the phone on speaker, Butch shut off the freaking music.

Hello, what the hell is going on Tim?

Joey, I was just stopped by the cops here on Park Street.

Did the cop say anything about the hydrant?

No he did not, Thank God.

Tony and I will meet you guys at Apple Tree Apartments see you in a little while.

Okay goodbye.

About twenty minutes later, I pulled into the back lot of the apartment. I could hear Nicky yelling at Joey from the other end of the parking lot. I drove the truck over to them, Nicky started yelling at us! As his hands went flying in every direction. We want all of you freaking knuckle head to get out of the f —-kin truck now. Nicky and Joey walked to the back of the truck to see the damage. Nicky was yelling at Joey in Italian. Joey answers him back in English. Don't worry about it. The truck will look new again I will make arrangement to get it fix right now. Then Joey got on his phone.

Nicky started asking question. So Tim what the hell had happen this morning to my truck?

Nicky I was backing up, got stuck on black ice, then the truck had slide to the right and hit the fire hydrant.

Tim by and chance were you drinking or smoking weed last night?

No Nicky I was not.

So where the hell were you guys? Didn't any one help Tim back in that alley?

Butch, tell me what had happen.

Well Nicky it was dark snowing and sleeting like crazy we could not see the black ice.

What do you have to say Victor?

The two streets lights at the stop in the alley way were out which it was hard for us to see?

Are you bullshitting me Victor?

No Nicky, go down Pearl Street... you will see what I mean. Sometimes the lights are left on all day. You know Nicky you don't believe a freaking word I say any ways.

Don't getta smart with me Victor? I will run your ass back to your home. The warden would love to get you back. Nicky started to lay into Victor yelling at him getting him madder. Then Victor kept on yelling back at Nicky. As they both kept on arguing with each other.

I can't believe Victor is saying that to Nicky.

Okay cut the crap Victor, Joey yelled out then he put his phone in his pocket.

Nicky, let these guys go back to work, they're running late.

Ok Joey let's go to Pearl Street and check out the lights. Then we can also look at the fire hydrant.

No Nicky too many cops are there, what are you freaking crazy? H E L L O!

Then Nicky gave Victor a mean look. Victor walked away laughing at Nicky.

Tim I want you to leave out these stops today,Jean's packages store, and vacuum store, world gifts, we will pick them up tomorrow. I want you in the yard by four with that truck empty as Joey yelled out top of his lungs.

Ok Joey, what about the bank last pickup today?

I will have the other crew take care of that. I don't want this truck down Pearl Street. I will see you later.

As I jumped into the truck I had asked Victor if there is really two lights out at the stop? Or were you bullshitting them.

Tim, I've been meaning to tell you that. I was side track with everything going on and I forgot to tell you.

The rest of the day was nerve racking every time I would hear a siren or see a cop car I would get so scare my hand were shaking and my nose was bleeding.

I kept on thinking the cops are coming after me.

The weather was crazy still snowing and sleeting and freezing out.

I got into the yard about three o'clock the guys left I went up to Joeys office to see him. Tim, Russ is going to fix the step now and paint the truck red. Russ will also paint one of the spare trucks red.

The cops are watching Pearl Street. In fact, I would bet that there is green paint from the step of the truck, is on to the fire hydrant now.

The cops are going to tried matching the color green. That's why I'm going to have Russ the welder work this weekend and paint the two trucks red they will never stop these trucks. You know any green truck going down Pearl Street is going to get pulled over.

Tim,Monday morning start your route on Canfield Avenue. If you get stop call me at once I will take care of it. I'm going to see my lawyer tomorrow morning early.

Okay Joey I'm really sorry. Son its ok just be more careful.

Good night I will see you Monday

Ok Joey Thank You.

CHAPTER NINE

RUN BUT YOU CAN'T HIDE

The next day things were going smooth, we were running on time. I pulled in the back parking lot at the vacuum shop. I quickly stopped the truck I was jumping out to grab the can, when I notice Butch was heading over to Mr. Pizza can.

He was picking up the empty boxes from the ground and threw them on top of the can rolling the can toward the truck.

Hey Butch, Mr. Pizza stop you know as well I know, it's not in the route book. This stop is not one of Joey's accounts.

Yo Tim, Listen dog. This is our route I'm getting a large pizza with everything on it for us in return for dumping his can.

Don't worry aren't you hungry?

Yes but I will pass. I'm not stealing from Joey and especially Nicky. So Butch roll that can back you're not dumping it!

Get the hell out of my way Tim.

Yo, Victor, listen to this joker telling me I can't dump this can! Ha! ha!. Come on Victor, we are not going to get caught.

Victor if you do get caught you will be going right back to the slammer and giving up all your freedom. You know as well as I do Joey will not hesitate to do that especially when Nicky hate's you. Victor is it worth stealing? Don't you like your freedom? We both know sooner or later you're going to get caught.

Victor started walking in a big circle looking down at the ground thinking about what I had just said.

Yo Victor screw Tim, do not listen to him. That boy is bullshitting you we will not get caught trust me. Bro look how long we have been doing it. We have it all under control dog. Victor we have a good thing going.

Butch, Tim is right.

I am not going back to the slammer for you or anyone else Dude.

Next thing to my surprise I felt a punch. Butch hit me on the right side of my face. I had hit the ground. I got up spitting blood out of my mouth and started to fight back.

I was able to get Butch in a headlock squeezing hard.

Butch, no more stealing I kept on yelling out to him.

Okay, Okay, Let me go.

I threw him to the ground and walked away.

Then I heard Victor yelled out Tim, watch out Butch has a knife in his hand!

I quickly turned my head to see what was going on.

Butch was running toward me and Victor is running right behind him yelling.

Dude, drop the knife, you're going to get hurt.

Victor leave us alone. Tim is mine.

I turned around to get ready for second round with Butch.

Victor had beaten me to the punch. He grabbed Butch hand and squeezed it hard until the knife he was holding hit the ground. Butch would not give up.

Victor was punching Butch as if he was a punching bag. He sure didn't lose his touch. Then Butch hit the ground hard in pain yelling and cursing.

Dude you better get the hell out of here by the time we get out of the store.

Tim, let's get something to drink.

We walked into the package store, the man behind the counter started to talk to us. Man it looks like you guys had a tough day already.

Yes sir your right

Son, you may use the bathroom, it's in the back of the store to wash your face, and it's pretty bloody.

Go ahead Tim we have time.

Okay, thank you sir.

I could hear just a little conversation Victor was having with the man.

Telling him what had happened with Butch and me.

I came out of the bathroom grabbed two cans of soda from the refrigerator put them on the counter. I was reaching in my pocket to get the money.

Those sodas are on me.

Thank you sir that's nice of you.

I respect an honest person today there are few too many that are not around. You both can work for me any time.

Thank you Sir, that's nice of you see you later.

No problem son, have a nice day.

Victor and I were walking to the truck, when we noticed there was Butch emptying the can in the truck from the pizza restaurant. Suddenly I felt a tunnel of wind past by us it had almost knocked me to the ground. This car came a little too close.

I turned around to curse at the driver as I was walking over to the car to give the driver a piece of my mind. The car door was thrown open before the car could stop. The driver jammed the car into park to make a complete stop. The car jerked back and forth with a loud grinding noise. Then a man stepped out of the car fast. It was Joey in a different car. Butch is caught in the act.

That is not one of my accounts Joey yelled at Butch this is one of your own many accounts you have hidden from me! So how much money is he giving you, to dump his can in my truck? How many free pizzas are you getting a week?

Butch, mouth had dropped open. He could not say a word he was in shocked.

I've been watching you for a while. I can't believe you're doing this to me. After I had saved your black ass so many freaking times. I gave you a job, which so many people are losing their jobs because of the economy, is turning for the worse. I paid you high wages. I provided your health insurance free to you, which I paid for out of my pocket. For you and all your kids that you have scratcher around,this freakin city because you can't keep your pecker in your pants.

You forgot all the times I had picked your ass up to come to work in the morning, because you're were out drugging or drinking all night,you can't get up or don't have a ride to work. What about the times I had lend you money with no interest to buy that nice car you wanted.

Remember you ended up totaling the last car because you can't stay away from the devils juice and drugs. You still owe me money for that last car loan. I also got you the best lawyer money can buy and I paid for him to keep your ass out of prison when you got caught for dealing drugs. Then you promise me that day you were going to clean up your act.

H E L L O.

Boy you must of got amnesia.

You forgot how good you did have it working for me.

So is this how you repay me?

By stealing from me?

Butch was speechless he quickly look all around trying to figure out what to do next. Then butch dropped the can that he just finished emptying, looked behind him at Joey and started to run away.

Joey ran over to the truck, picked up the metal can that Butch had just dumped. He held the can sideways, one hand was on the top of the can, and the other hand grabbed the bottom of the can. He lifted up the can and put the can behind his head aimed it at Butch then through it in the air. You could hear a whistle as the air travel through the bottom of the can where the holes were. Then Joey started yelling in Italian at Butch. The can landed in front of butch's path right where he was running.

There was no way that Butch could have dodged that can. It was a perfect lucky throw. Butch fell over the can head first face down and slide on the asphalt, yelling and cursing! Piece of asphalt were stuck in his face, he was bleeding bad. That boy was in serious pain.

Do not bother coming to the yard for your pay check next week, its mine now. Never use me or my company for a job reference. I'm through with you.

Joey was so pissed that his veins were ready to pop out of his neck he then turned around and looked at Victor and I and yelled out.Victor that better not be a can of beer you're drinking in that brown bag you're holding.

Victor didn't say a word. He looked like he was in another world, very puzzled not believing what he just saw happened.

You know there is no drinking on the job. I told you once before. I want to see both of you in my office after you finish your route.

Yes Sir.

Joey walked fast to his car slammed the door took off and laid a patch of rubber about ten feet long you know that man is ripping.

Tim this is not a coincidence that Joey was here.

You're right. I think he had been watching us for a while.

Dam if that's the case Joey also saw me with Butch emptying those other can. Crap I don't want to go back to the slammer. I'm afraid Joey may send me back. All he has to do is make a call to my probation officer and I'm through.

I could tell Victor was scared to see Joey.

Tim I need help what should I do?

Whatever you say Victor don't lie to Joey.

You better hope that Nicky is not in that meeting with you and Joey.

Dude, you got that right.

Tim, do you have any good idea that could help me out?

I have to think about that, let's get this last stop then hit the dump and head in.

Oh crap.

What's wrong Tim?

It is starting to snow and the roads are getting slippery.

Bud, we will be in the yard before you know it. Tim turn the heat on its cold in this truck my nuts are freezing.

You got it Victor.

So Tim what should I do? Bud you know Joey better than I do.

I don't know what to tell him were almost at the yard.

Tim take a left. I do not want to go in just yet.

Victor I drove around the block three times already. I really need to go in now. I have class tonight. I need to get my ass home I'm sorry.

I pulled the truck into the yard, when a man that I never seen before was yelling at me in a rude voice. As if, I had did something wrong to pissed him off. Bring the truck here now he was screaming at me.

Victor rolled his window down. Hey Dude, what is your freaking problem man? Tim I don't like the way he was yelling at us. That Dude has attitude which I'm going to fix now.

Victor, you're in a lot of trouble as it is now forget him.

It was too late, by the time the words forget him came out of my mouth Victor was already out of the truck having words with the Dude. They were both arguing with each other, Victor is getting more ma., he jacked that boy up against the wall with one hand and the other hand was in a tight fist getting ready to throw a punch at the Dude.

Victor don' t hit him he's not worth it. I yelled out.

Please let me go. The Dude was begging for his life. Man I'm sorry.

Victor threw the guy to the ground.

Then he started yelling out to him Dude. If I should ever here that you talk to anyone again like you did to us. I will kick your Italian white ass from here to kingdom come. Then victor walked away.

Yo Victor what's happening man?

Not much Spikes it been a really ugly bad day.

Dog, do you know who the boy is you just jacked up against the wall over there?

Nope and I don't freaking care.

That boy needs to shut his freaking mouth. You are right on that.

Dog you better have a seat. You're too big for me to pick up from the ground. He started laughing out loud. (L O L) That is Nicky's boy.

What are you talking about Spike?

That is Nicky's grandson.

I don't care if that was the Vice President son.

That Dude should not be so freaking rude.

Dog your right. I'm not disagreeing with you. I'm just letting you know Nicky will be calling your ass on the carpet.

Dog we are not talking about the red carpet you were used to in your younger day either. Ha! ha.!

Your good Spike you haven't lost your sense of humor. Thanks Spike for the scoop. I got to go to see Joey now.

Yes Victor, I got to go and see if they finished fixing my truck? My new helper hit a bus today and messed up the front fender of our truck, he is upstairs talking to Joey and Tony now.

Oh shit that's just great he's getting those two guys primed up for my meeting dam.

Victor, are you alright man? I never see you pissed off like this before.

Yo, Dog I'm good later Spike.

I knocked on Joeys door, hoping he have left for the day.

No such luck.

Come in.

You wanted to see me sir?

Yes Tim, have a seat.

I see you have a big cut on your face.

I'm ok.

I wanted to thank you for what you did sticking up for my company and stopping the stealing from those guys. You know I have been watching you guys for a few weeks.

I had heard from one of Butch's private customer the Chicken Coop Restaurant. The owner of the Restaurant's son, Jake called my office for a pickup. His father was in the hospital not knowing what was going on. Jake's father and Butch had an agreement going on between them, dumping the restaurant trash. His father was giving Frankie, Butch, Victor free lunch twice a week. Plus cash three hundred dollars a month. I wanted to see who else was involved and how many accounts there were stealing from us. I know of fifteen accounts so far.

I'm aware of what's going on. Your crew was stealing before I hired you. We fired the last driver Frankie because he was stealing. That's why we hire you, to take over his route. You know Tim?

A few month ago Nicky, was having lunch at T J Italian Giant Grinders on Wethersfield Avenue. He was sitting at the counter looking outside the window, eating a big beef cutlet grinder,when he saw from across the street Frankie stopped the truck. Butch jumped out and rolled a full eight yard trash can down the driveway to the truck which was parked on the street to empty it. This was not one of our accounts.

Then the owner from the Meat Market walked down to the street to the truck. He talked to Frankie as he handed a wad of money plus a large, Styrofoam cooler, which we found out later there were three big ribeye steaks on ice. Nicky could not believe what he was seeing.

So, after Frankie drove away Nicky walked over to the meat market. He found the man that handed Frankie the cash and the cooler. Nicky found out all the information. We got smart and started to follow all our trucks for months to see what stops the crews had on their own.

They never knew we had been watching them. We always drive around different type of cars, so no one would recognize us. We even took video of these guys stealing. They never knew they were on camera.

We did this in case we had to go to court, we were prepared.

The amount of money we were losing a month was over four thousand dollars. There is going to be more drivers and helpers getting fired within the next few days. Tim, this conversation, is between me and you no one can know.

Joey I won't say a word.

Tim, I can't thank you enough for being honest. I'm going to increase your pay by one hundred dollars more a week starting right now. If there is anything you want Tim? You got it. How's, school doing?

Good,it's just been hard but I just keep on plugging along.

Tim I want you to go after were through here to the medical center down the street, And have that cut on your face taking care of.

You will see a pretty dirty blond tall skinny girl in the front office her name is Tracie. Tim she is the billing manager nice girl, tell her to bill me.

Ask her to put you in the front of the waiting line, tell her you're in a hurry you have to go. Tim also mention to her I will be by to see her.

Okay Joey I will.

Tim this is also for you. He handed me two fresh new one hundred bills. Merry Christmas.

Thank you, Joey.

Tim if there is anything I can do for you let me know?

There are two things I wanted to ask you for?

Go ahead Tim what do you want?

It's not any of my business I know but, please don't send Victor back to prison.

There must be a way of working it out.

Your right Tim there is a way to work this out. Victor needs to go back to prison he is a freaking thief. Joey yelled out so loud that I'm sure everyone in the building heard him, that's a hard request to do. I'm not going to promise you anything Tim. And the other request?

I need to take some time off from work. I'm going to Mississippi for two weeks.

You got it Tim.

Tim, just let me know about three weeks in advance for your trip so I can get someone to cover your route when you're gone.

Okay thank you.

Joey, Merry Christmas.

Thank you, Tim. Oh, by the way Tim.

You are going to have a new helper Monday.

Okay thanks.

I just open the door to leave I saw Victor coming up the hall. We both waved to each other.

I was waiting for the elevator to come up and I could hear Joey yelling at Victor. I walked in to the elevator as I looked through the glass in the elevator noticed Nicky was walking fast in the hallway heading to Joeys' office.

Thank god. I finally got out of there.

I stopped at the medical office. It was full, not a seat was empty. I walked over to the counter and sign in. I asked the lady at the desk if I could please see Trace.

Sure go down the hall first left is her office. I will tell her you're on your way, your name is?

Tim Ripper

Trace started laughing when I said to her that Joey, will be by to see her.

Okay Tim your next in line.

The nurse ended up putting eight stitches in the right side of my face. Then I headed straight home in pain and went to bed.

Chapter Ten

Slugger
===✦===

Its Saturday morning 7:00 am I've been trying to study for my exam for the last two hours, but it is it too hard. I was not really in the mood. I just could not concentrate too many things were bugging me. I could not help but wonder how Victor made out with Joey and Tony. Will Joey send Victor back to prison or will he give him another chance I had sent two text messages and called Victor's phone a few times and left a few messages for him to call me back, but I never heard from him.

Twenty minutes later my phone was ringing it was Duke he was checking in with me. He wanted to see if I needed anything. Then he was filling me in on what was going on with him and the members. The club got six new members that bring the total up to sixty two members. He said the fee went up fifty dollars more for new member which now is two hundred fifty. He will send me out a check for six hundred twenty dollars. He wants me to invest it for him.

The newest news is that Mr. Carter had a heart attack last week driving home from the bar he passed out and hit a telephone pole and died. I asked him how the Doctor is doing. To my surprise they had split up. He asked me how I was doing with school and I told him good and in May is when I'm going to graduate. He was so happy for me. Duke mentions that he and some of the members were coming to my graduation.

He mentioned that he will be my first client, the club wanted me to represent them, with all their legal matters. Sure, I told him you got it.

That night I just could not sleep I kept tossing and turning, I got up at 2am, showered and left the house, stopped to see Sue and chat with her for a while, grabbed a hot coffee. I was at the yard at 4:30am. I went under the truck checking out a small puddle, hoping it was not an oil leak. It was water. Thank God. I heard the garage door slammed, footsteps walking toward the truck. Hey Victor how is it going Bud? You're here early. What's up with that?

Excuse me I'm looking for Tim. I thought Victor was clowning around, changing his voice, acting like a sexy young lady. As I stared to pull myself up from under the truck, a hand reached out to help pull me up. I picked my head up. I could not believe what I was seeing in front of me.

Are you alright?

Yes Miss Thanks.

My name is Tammy Grace. It's nice to meet you. Likewise, my name is Tim Ripple. Tim I am your new helper.

Cool,Victor is our helper he should be here any minute.

Tammy I would have to say she looked in her early twenties. She has long red hair, brown eyes, beautiful face with freckles she looked like an actress on TV. She is hot to trot very pretty girl 6ft inch tall, slim, and muscular with a tight body, no fat. You could tell she works out. When she talked, it was so obvious she was very educated. She was not from the streets.

Tammy what bring you here to this company?

Joey is good friends with my Dad for over twenty five years. Dad and three of my brothers started a rubbish company about six years ago in New Haven.

Why don't you work for your father?

I wanted to, but Dad and I don't see eye to eye. To this day he is still pissed at me? He's from the old school he just doesn't understand me.

I had to ask her why?

I went to four years of college for journalism and graduated with high honors. I worked for a local TV news station as a reporter for the news for three years.

Sounds like a great job.

I was getting burned out the hours killed me. I started at 2:00am to 11:00 am six days a week. The money was great. I had no life so I left. Pop does not understand me. He thinks that I should have stayed at the TV station. I saw Joey at my cousins wedding three weeks ago.

Tony, Joey and I were talking, they both knew I just left the TV station and had no job.

Joey offered me a job in the office. Then I asked him if he could put me on a truck instead. He laughed and laughed. I told him I was serious I wanted to be a helper and a driver I had asked Joey if he would help me get my CDL license. I'm tired of office work. I know Joey would talk to Dad and asked if it be ok to work for him. Dad said sure. Here I am.

A loud screaming voice yelling through the garage Yo Tim are you still here bro?

Yes, Victor over here.

Boy I'm happy to see you.

Same back at you Bro.

Victor I called and text you but you never replied. What happen?

Sorry my phone dropped in the sink fill with water when I was washing dishes. It was destroyed sorry I could not get back to you.

Victor this is our new helper Tammy Grace.

It's nice to meet you Tammy.

Hey, aren't you the boxer Victor Gomez the Slugger? I know that's you.

Yes I am.

Man, I can't believe this. I love boxing. I'm a great fan of your. I got to call Dad tonight and tell him.

Let's get out of here before Joey or Nicky comes here. Nicky is still pissed at me Tim is the truck ready to go?

Yes Victor.

Wow! I saw you fight Jimmy Lopez in New Haven at the coliseum many years ago.

Your right, that was me young lady.

I have to tell you Slugger. I thought that you were knocked out in the third round. You surprised everyone. I remember, you got back up and your face was cover with blood. Your right eye was cut bad you could not see well.

Dam girl you really know that fight well.

You could just about walk. You were tripping on your own feet. Then you were grabbing the rope trying hard to stay up staggering and heading for Lopez. You started yelling something out at him. I could not understand what the hell you were saying.

Then you started to do your famous shuffle dance and jab, next you hit Lopez so hard with an upper right hook and knocked him out cold. Dad told me a lot of people lost big bucks over you. They thought you would never get up and it was over for you, not knowing that you were going to kicked Lopez ass then she started to laugh.

Victor was that one of your hardest fight?

Sweetheart you got that right.

Sweetheart the boys said. I started to laugh, thinking to myself this is one of Victors' favorite lines for picking up the ladies.

Lopez is a great fighter. In fact I talked to him two weeks ago at the gym. He is doing well. He is heading back home to the Philippines. He won the title three weeks ago. He just got paid last week he told me.

Hey Slugger can you show me how to do your famous shuffle.

Sure Tammy follow me, it goes like this. You're getting the moves girl just like that, now just move your left foot a little more back like this. Throw a right punch to my face. Then bend your head to the left to your shoulder and don't take your eyes off of me.

You got it girl.

Dam Tim this beautiful young lady knows who I am.

But you don't H E L LO. What the hell is up with that?

Hey Victor can you show Tammy the move on how to roll that can to the truck.

HA! ha! You're very funny Tim.

So Victor what happen Friday? I went up to see Joey he told me to go to Nicky's office he will be there shortly. I walked into Nicky office there was my probation officer Terry Wall along with a prison guard sitting there listening to Nicky ratting me out.

Before, I could say a freaking word Joey walked into Nicky's office for our meeting he was shocked. Joey started yelling at Nicky what the hell is going on here?

Well I called Terry and told him to take Victor back, the warden can deal with him. I'm through putting up with Victor crap. You would think by now he had learned, but no he didn't.

Then Joey started screaming at Nicky in Italian. As his hands started to fly and the spit was coming out of his mouth.

They both keep on arguing back and forth. But for some reason Joey stood up for me. He told them he would take care of this problem. That I'm going to pay them back. He starting yelling at me you owe us a lot of money. Then he gives me a big speech in front of everyone.

You will report to Russ the welder on Saturdays 7:00 am and you will work eight hours painting cans all freaking day for no pay.

Do, you hear me Victor? I said no pay we will keep track of your hours you work. When you pay us back in full from the money you stole from us, having your own accounts then you can stop coming in working on Saturdays. Your hourly rate for Saturdays is going to be straight time, not time in a half. If there is one Saturday you miss without permission. Terry will tracked your ass down you will be behind bars within hours. Trust me Victor. Then Joey says I'm not playing with you.

Nicky started yelling again. He was stuttering badly with his broken English.That boy was ripening.

But Joey just ignored him.

Then Nicky told me if there is any more problem you're out of here in a heartbeat. Then you will finish your prison term.

What do you have to say for yourself?

I understand you both I told them.

Then Joey apologized for Nicky calling them. He told them there was a miscommunication problem between them. Joey tells Terry while you're here I want to ask you I need a few more workers. Can you get me a few?

Sure I have three guys getting out on parole next week. Two of them have their CDL licenses I will send them to you.

Then Joey thanked him and said oh here is something for both of you guy.

Victor, what did Joey give them? He gave then both a gift card for fifty dollars for the new restaurant on Silver Lane Charles Steak House they were happy. As I was leaving the meeting, Nicky tells me to leave his grandson alone.

Victor what do you mean leave Nicky's grandson alone?

Dog you know when I walked over to the truck washer and jacked up that kid with the big mouth.

Dude you aren't going to tell me that was his grandson!

H E L L O

Bro you got it he is.

You got to be kidding me.

No I'm not joking that boy calls Pops up and complained about me.

I'm glad I had listened to you. When you told me don't hit him.

Me too.

By the way Tim, Joey told for me to thank you personally. That man told me that you ask him not to send me back. I owe you big time Bro. No Dude we are all set.

Tammy I'm sorry I didn't mean to be rude I just had to tell Tim what went on.

No problem Victor I understand.

I know how you boys love to gossip. Then Tammy started laughing.

You're going to fit in just right young lady.

As the day went on things were going good, we all were getting along fine. As weeks, months went by Tammy was learning the route and did all the driving. She was going for her test for her CDL license in a few weeks. Victor and I were hanging out on the back of the truck talking laughing and listening to music.We were having a great time.

One day we were picking up a stop when out of the blue Tammy asked Victor if he could teach her boxing. Victor told her that he would but the Gym was in the bad part of town. Victor told her he didn't really want her there. The north end of Hartford Flaming Street is a rough neighborhood which is in the middle of the ghetto. Crime is bad there. She told him that she was not afraid. There was bad part of New Haven she had to deal with all the time, reporting, killing, drug dealer, rapes, shooting etc. So Victor decided to bring her to the gym and started training her. Being with Victor all the time around the gym people were talking. People showed her respect. Tammy is very easy going.

Months went by Joey ended up getting those new customers that Butch and Victor once had. Victor was happy coaching Tammy she was thrill, she had her CDL license life was looking good. Tammy had asked Victor if he could set up a fight for her, in New Haven. Victor tries talking her out of it. But could not he has a kind heart.

I could tell that Tammy and Victor were starting to be more than just good friend. I was not the only one noticing it. Tammy would drop Victor off on Saturday morning to work. Then she would come back to bring lunch and stay with him and leave after lunch then pick him up after work. Then they both went to the gym they were inseparable.

Life for me was going good I had just pass my last exam with a b+ now the ending was coming I been studying hard for my bar exam that was coming up in two month. I just could not wait.

Chapter Eleven

Mistaken

The weekend is here. It was Saturday 5pm I pulled up to Linda's house blowing the horn. Linda stuck her head out the window and yelled out I will be out in a minute Tim. I was turning the knob on the radio trying to find a good station to listen to,when I looked out my window and notice there was a huge black German shepherd barking charging toward me. I was able to close the window just in time as the dog started to jump on to my truck started growling at me as he watched me thru the window, scratching the paint on my truck door with its long nails. His saliva was all over my window you could tell this dog was not playing he wants me bad.

Then I heard Mr. Star yelling, Prince get down now boy. Bad boy

Tim I got him.

Thank you, Mr. Star.

I'm sorry about that Tim.

Are you ok?

Your face is white, like you saw a ghost.

Do you need to go home and change your pants?

Ha! ha!

That was a good one Mr. Star.

Tim I could always tell my daughter you have forgot your license. Then he started laughing. I'm only joking Tim. I'm sorry about the scratches on the door. Get it painted and bring me the bill. I will take care of it. Prince is going to start walking the beat with me Monday. He is actually a great narcotic dog. What a nose on him.

Does Linda like Prince?

Ha! ha! That's another story.

Hello Tim.

Hey Linda that's a nice outfit you're wearing.

Thanks Tim.

Dad, I will be home later, Tim and I are going out for dinner.

Dad you could please keep that monster away from my cats?

Thanks, Dad.

Dam it I just drop and smash my cell phone in the house. Now it won't work. Dad, Kenny may call the house phone since he can't call me on my cellphone. Could you please tell him I will see him tomorrow?

Sure sweetheart no problem.

Thanks Dad.

Oh Dad I just made you spaghetti for dinner its hot on the table go and eat before it gets cold.

Okay sweetheart thank you. Both of you have a nice time.

Wait a minute Dad?

What did you forget now?

Dad, I made a fresh batch of meat balls yesterday for your spaghetti dinner today. And also you can have meatball grinder for lunch tomorrow.

Dad the meatball is gone. Did you eat them?

No but Prince did. Ha! ha!

That's very funny Dad.

Dad, I can't believe you gave him my meatball. I worked so hard making them for you not the dog.

I'm sorry sweetheart I was in a hurry. I ran out of dog food so I gave him the meatballs don't get mad.

Dad, never do this again.

Okay sweetheart see you guys later have a nice dinner bye.

Let's get out of here Tim.

Linda how is this guy Kenny?

I know you will like him he is so nice.

That's cool its sound like you're in love.

Maybe I really do care for him.

Tim how are you doing?

Good.

Tim, where are we going for dinner?

How about at Dell's Surf and Turf Restaurant .

That sounds good Tim.

The restaurant was packed. I have finally found a parking space after driving around looking for an empty space for the last fifteen minutes.

Good evening how many in your party?

Two please.

You're in luck there is an empty table follow me in the other room, next to the window, with a great view of the airport. Follow me, here you are.

Thank You Sir.

Hello I will be your waitress my name is Jean.

What can I get you to drink?

I will have a stinger on the rocks.

And what can I get you sir?

I will have an ice tea with a piece of lemon without sugar please.

Sure.

Thank you.

I will be right back with your drinks then I will take your order.

Okay thank you Jean.

So Tim have you been studying for the bar exam?

I have been trying to. It just a lot of things have been happening in my life, I need to crack down and study more.

By the way Linda your graduation was nice.

Thanks for going. I can't believe I'm an RN it took me four years. I will be starting my new job Monday, second shift 3:00pm – 11:00pm.

Where?

At Saint Mary's Hospital on the fifth floor the Cancer floor. Tim speaking of cancer did you know that Mr. White has colon cancer?

No I was not aware.

Linda when did you find this out?

Three weeks ago.

That was around the same time around when he helped me moved to my home and he never said a word about this to me.

Tim he didn't want to tell you. He wanted to keep it a secret. Mr. White knows you will be upset. He is going to have chemo treatment in two weeks. Tim did you know that Judge Bailey is retiring Feb10th this year 2014? No, but that's good news.

Tim my lawsuit trial is March 5 that is perfect timing I'm so happy Judge Bailey is leaving. He has so much pull in the court system. Now I will have a greater chance to win my case. I'm still paying for my medical bills. Did you hear the latest news Judge Bailey grandson Mark Heal, the killer was just arrested last week for selling heroin? Dad told me. Let see if he get off this time.

Tim when I had talked to you a few months ago you mention you were thinking of going on vacation.

Yes, I went to Mississippi for two weeks.

Did you say Mississippi?

Yes it was different.

Tim what the hell is in Mississippi?

A stinger for you young lady and here is your ice tea young man.

Are you ready to order?

Yes, we are.

What would you like miss?

Whole belly fried clams please.

You have two side dishes comes with your dinner. Would you like fries or bake potato, peas, or corn?

Fries and corn please and I would like extra tartar sauces and lemon thanks.

Sir what can I get you?

I will have a rib eye steak cooked well-done, fries, and peas.

Thank you I will place you order in now, is there anything else I can get you?

No, we are good for now thank you.

Wait till you see our desserts? We have a black raspberry cheese cake, chocolate cream pie, red velvet cake they're all so delicious. You two may help yourself to the salad bar the dishes are up there. Okay thanks Linda you can go first I will stay here and watch your pocket book.

Okay thanks.

I was waiting for Linda to get back. I started to daydream about my trip from Mississippi. Then I heard a loud voice yelling Tim how's it going bud?

Then a deep jolly laugh so loud that when he laugh everyone around started laughing even strangers were laughing at his laugh. Hey Tony how's is it going?

Just great this is my wife Carmen.

It's nice to meet you.

Tim I feel like I already know you. I heard nice things about you. Oh my father in law Joey can't help talking about you, he really respect you.

Thank you,that's nice to hear.

Then Tony introduces his daughter Constance nice to meet you. And as you notice my wife has one in the oven.

Dad, please don't say one in the oven, Mom does not like that right Mom? Okay sweetheart I will not say that any more. Ha! ha!

Linda this is Tony my boss Joey's son.

Hello this is my wife Carmen and my daughter Constance. It's Nice to meet all of you.

When are you due?

April 10 th.

Congratulation!

I'm hoping for a son.

Tony already bought his favorite football team shirts for the baby. He said the baby is going to be a boy.

I told him to stop buying boys clothes. It could be a girl we don't know yet. I don't want him to be pissed.

I'm so happy for you.

Thank you. We better get back to our table our friends are wondering where we went to.

Okay see you guys later?

Tim go ahead get some salad.

Sure thanks.

As we were enjoying our dinner Linda had a look on her face like something was wrong.

Are you ok?

Yes.

Is the dinner ok?

Yes, it's delicious thanks

Linda what's wrong?

Tim something is not right here.

Listen it's so quite in here, if you look outside the parking lot there are six policemen sitting in their police cars waiting.

Maybe someone is going to have a baby?

No, there is no ambulance out there.

Maybe there is someone famous eating here.

Yea maybe you're right.

Tim you were going to tell me about you vacation in Mississippi

I'm sorry sure.

Tim, are you ok?

Yes why?

Your, nose is bleeding.

Dam it, not again.

Here's a napkin hold you head looking down, then take two fingers and squeeze you nose that will stop the bleeding fast. Tim I have been noticing over to the left corner of the room there is a couple talking to each other but they keep on looking at us. A few minutes later I heard a loud voice say.

Excused me, Sir is your name Tim Ripple?

Yes sir it is.

And who are you guys?

We are with the F. B. I you are wanted for the murder of Joe Hall. Then he handed me his cell phone that had a photo of Joe Hall lying in a puddle of blood in the ally with the date, time, place.

Okay guys the joke is over.

Who the hell put you two up to do this?

Tim this is no joke. Do you hear us laughing? Tim why were you in Mississippi about six weeks ago?

I went on vacation.

Take a good look at this man Joe Hall.

I'm happy the creep is dead, but I did not kill him.

After our fight, Joe got up from the ground and walked away. I went to the hospital to get my leg fixed. Someone else had killed him after I left that night.

Tim your fingerprints were all over his clothes you were the last one to be seen with him.

I'm thinking to myself, oh this is great now Linda thinks I'm a killer.

Yes there is definitely a mistake here I didn't kill anyone. I was trying to get up from my seat thinking maybe I can talk these guy into going outside to finish this bizarre conversation.

Have a seat the lady shouted at me as she stood behind me and started pushing me back down into the seat.

I'm not going to say anything more, until I see my lawyer.

I'm so in embarrassed. The restaurant is quiet; people stopped talking and eating they were just listening to what we were saying, their eyes staring at us. I could tell that Linda was in shock by the way she was looking at me.

Excuse me people but I'm going to the ladies room. Linda got up from the table and started walking away she stopped quickly turned her body around, fainted and fell on top of a full table of six.

Dishes, glasses, cups silverware all went flying from the table to the floor what a loud crashing sound. What a mess, food scattered all over the place, from the table, to the window, to the floor. It looked like one big food fight went on.

The restaurant went from silent to chaos people yelling and screaming. As you heard different conversations. This coffee is hot it burned my leg what the hell is going on?

Young Lady please get up, what is wrong with you? Then I notice a lady yelling and shaking Linda.

Waiter! Waiter!

Yes

Honey I believe the girl is dead. She is not moving at all.

Mom, look at my new suit, melted butter all over it.

Daddy look at my new dress, it's full of cocktail sauce. I will never be able to get it cleaned. Mary let me wipe your face you also have some cocktail sauce all over it. This suck's Dad this is my favorite dress. Sweetheart watched your language please.

Then a man walk fast over to the table that Linda fell on.

Is everyone ok here?

I'm sorry for what had happen! Let's all leave this table. I have a new table for you in the other room in the back.

Hey Sir, What about taking care of our clothes? They're ruined.

I will buy new clothes for you guys no problem, and dinner is on me for all the trouble you people have been through.

My name is Jeff Dill, I'm the owner, follow your waiter. Excuse me young man may I please use your cell phone? I need to call for an ambulance right away.

Sure go ahead Mr. Dill

Thank you.

A lady from across the aisle, the third table down was screaming and yelling her lungs out.

Help! Help!

There is a prosthetic foot that hit me in the head and landed on my plate. Miss I will be right there.

Tim Ripple, you are under arrest for killing Joe Hall. Before I could say another word, the F B I woman had quickly grabbed both my hands yanked them behind my back and cuffed me fast. Then she rambles on my rights. To my surprise the lady had pulled out her gun put it against my back and told me walk slowly.

Hey Miss put that dam gun away. I'm not going to take off. There are a lot of families with kids here. They don't need to see this.

Paula before you take him outside could you please grabbed both of their glasses and silverwares we will use them for DNA testing.

Bobby did you want the young lady too?

Yes take it all.

She may also be involved in the murder with him.

I got them.

Hey Miss what the hell are you doing? I'm the owner here. You can't take my glasses and silverware. You are stealing them. Those are mine.

She flashed her badge in front of his face and told him in a rude voice, you will get them back after the trial is over.

Miss please take him out the backdoor. My restaurant is going to be the talk of this town. I had a line of people out there in the front waiting to get in. Because of all the police cars in my parking lot, and with all the commotion going on in here, all the people left and there is nobody waiting to be seated anymore its dead.

As I was walking by the owner I yelled out. Sir here is my bill.

Then he took my bill put it up to his face, his hands was shaken so bad. He was so nervous after hearing the conversation at the table he might of thought, that I was going to kill him and skip out on the bill.

Sir please take the money out of my top left pocket and keep the change I'm. sorry this happen here and for the record sir. I'm not a killer. Thank you

Tim is everything ok?

No Tony.

This sucks! I'm accused of murder and I didn't do it.

How can I help you?

Please,could you help Linda out? They are taking her to the hospital. She will need a ride home. Also can you please bail me out of jail?

Yeah no problem Tim.

CHAPTER TWELVE

SURPRISE

I've been here two weeks in this hell hole! It's getting crazy guys are arguing and fighting over things like space. I just wanted to be left alone.

The jail cell was overcrowded, besides the noise, bad strong B O smell. I was bending over to tie my sneaker, when I heard a loud voice yelled at me.

Hey Dude where are you from?

I pretended not to hear him. I was in no mood to talk to anyone.

Yo, Dude I, know you're not from Connecticut?

And how is that I answered him.

By that tattoo on your left arm Desert Kings. You're from Detroit Michigan. Are you a member of that club?

Yea

My, ex-brother in law has the same tat as you.

What's the dude's name?

Raymond Larson.

I don't know him.

He hangs with his best friend Duke. They're like brothers, they were both in the service and fought overseas together.

Is this guy big?

Yes, that boy calls him Tiny.

Yes I know you ex brother-in-law good. Tiny is a good friend of mine.

So Dude what are you in here for?

Drugs, fighting or child support.

None of the above Dude.

I'm in here for murder!

Did you just say murder?

Yea Dude that right f — — murder.

I remember Duke use to tell me Tim whenever you're in a bad, environment, or situation, you must change your attitude, fast, act like them. You will always survive. Street smarts son!

Just as I said murder the noise in the cell had stopped. I could hear the man from across the cell breaking wind. People that were crowding me had moved quickly away, I now had plenty of room, mouths had dropped and eyeballs just kept staring at me, waiting to hear about how I had killed someone. I just gave everyone a mean look, and it worked no one had asked me any more question they were all so scared of me.

I keep on thinking I just can't wait to get the hell out of here. Where is Tony he is supposed to put up my bail? I am so tired of too many sleepless nights.

It seemed like every hour the guard would call out names. Their bail came through. Just as fast these guys were leaving the cell; the guard would bring more guys in. The max is only twenty people they were up to twenty-eight and over crowded.

Just when I was dozing off, I heard a guard calling me Tim Ripple your out of here.

Thank you Sir.

Hey killer, tell Tiny I said hello my name is Jim O'Neal

I sure will Jim.

Thanks good luck with your case.

Then the guard told me go down the hall on the right side the first door on the left you need to sign you released paper.

Okay thanks.

As I went on my way, wondering who had bailed me out Tony, Linda or Joey.

There was not one of the three people in the office waiting for me, I was wondering where they were.

Are you Tim Ripper? Yes Sir.

I need your signature on these papers and you're out of here. Here are your belongings.

Excuse me sir, I'm missing my watch, and my blue star sapphire gold ring, along with my gold chain and cross.

They're at the lab in New Haven having a DNA test done on them.

That's just great.

So when can I expect to get my belonging back? Not until after the trial is over.

That really sucks.

You are right young man. It does sucks!

Here are your copies. Your court date is here in Connecticut May 15, 2014 at the courthouse on Washington Street in Hartford at 9:00 am. Not the courthouse on Washington Street in New Haven. People get confuse all the time. Here's a little advice take it for what it is worth. Don't skip bail, and don't show up late. I hear judge Jade is tough. You don't want to piss her off.

Ok Sir, thanks for that info.

Hello Tim, there you are. Son are you ok?

Yes, I am fine. Mrs. White what are you doing here? Where is Mr. White? Is he in the car waiting for us?

No son I hate to tell you this, and then she stopped talking as tears started to rolled down her face. Mr. White had passed away Tuesday night.

No way! I can't believe he is gone. What happened?

Mr. White was *in* so much pain, the cancer was getting worse. I rushed him to the hospital. Tim, Mr.White kept on asking to see you. Doctor gave him a shot of morphine. I tried to bail you out sooner but the courthouse claimed your paper work was lost. Every day I went down to the court house to see if they found them. Finally after two weeks the paperwork was found. It was too late Mr. White had passed away; as I read your paper work I noticed Judge Baily had signed them. Judge Bailey is getting us back from the embarrassment we made for him, and our lawsuit we finally won last month against his nephew.

That bastard, because of his stupid and childish games I was not there for Mr. White.

Tim I'm sorry.

It's not your fault.

I hugged Mrs. White I could not hold back the tears from coming out. Here was a man that I loved like a father, I have so many great memories of us together.

As I held her hand and tried to talk, the words that I was trying to say would not come out, I was speechless and choked up. I just can't believe Mr. White is gone! I could have spent the last few minutes with him.

Mrs White when is the service?

Tonight at 7:00 pm at O'Leary funeral home in Wethersfield.

Tim let's get out of here.

Ok.

How is Linda doing? After that day she must be mad at me?

No Tim she's not.

She is doing fine

Mrs White could you please drop me off at my place, I need to get clean up I just can't wait to jump in that hot shower. Boy do I need one bad.

Sure Tim.

Mrs White I just wanted to let you know, I did not kill anyone. Tim you don't have to explain to me son. We both know that.

I walked in my home it was like walking into a tornado the house was trashed. All my clothes and books, papers, and my beautiful paintings that were hanging on the wall are now broken on the floor. My mattress was dragged from the bed room to the living room. The only neat place was the kitchen where the search warrant was left on the table.

I was cleaning up the house and listening to my phone messages.

Tim call me back Joey.

Tim I'm sorry to hear about Mr. White I want to help you out Tim call me Duke.

Tim I hope you're ok? You had miss the bar exam last Tuesday call me Professor James.

Hey Tim I'm sorry what had happen? Call me I need to talk to you Linda. Tim call me please, Joey. I called Duke First I wanted to explain to him what had happened, and ask him if he could please help me. I only have a few weeks before my trial starts.

I faxed Duke all the information he needed. He said he would head out to Mississippi to investigate the murder the next day. I went down the list I decided not to call Tony or Joey I will just go into the office to talk to them. My last call was to Professor James. So I called him back hello Professor James.

Well hello Tim how are you doing?

I'm hanging in there.

I've been reading up on your case.

Man what a case.

You have been in all newspapers, TV and radio stations you're a celebrity. Have you received any book offers yet? Then he laughed.

No, I have been framed for a murder that I never committed.

Sir, I was wondering can I take my bar exam next week? I've been studying like crazy I'm ready for it. I know I will pass it with flying colors.

I'm sure you will Tim.

I'm sorry to say no that the next exam is in October, six month in this state, its offer twice a year.

New Orleans offers the Bar Exam three times a year. I'm sorry Tim I have no control over it.

Tim, we both know you have to win your case, clear you name before this state will let you take the bar exam.

Do you have an attorney?

No not yet.

If you want I would love to represent your case at no charge.

Pro Bono.

Yes I would like that but I want to pay you.

No, Tim I will do it free in return later when your acquitted and you pass your bar exam we will be partners open are own law office together.

Wow that sound good Professor James, Ok, thanks I will talk to you later.

Just as I hung up the phone the doorbell rang I really did not want to answer it, I was wondering who is it after me now. But I did, Hey Linda come in.

Thank you.

Tim, are you all right?

Yes I'm trying to hang in there

Linda how are you doing?

Good Tim.

I'm sorry about, Tim stop forget it, I understand what happen.

Oh by the way here is you cell phone. I had grab it put it in my purse thinking it was my phone.

I forgot, I left my phone at home. You know the Y-phones all looks a like.

Thank you.

Tim your phone was ringing like crazy and you have twenty text messages.

Boy I'm glad you grabbed it instead of the FBI.

Would you like for me to help you clean up?

No I'm all set thanks anyway.

Tim I have to go. One more thing, did Mrs. White tell you the good news? No she didn't.

She said she wanted to talk to me after the service. So Linda tell me what's the good news I sure could use some.

Mrs. White and I had our final hearing on the lawsuit case against Judge Bailey's grandson Mark Heal and we won. Because of him Johnny is gone and so is my leg.

I'm still having a hard time dealing with this but anyway Mrs. White received a check for 4.1 million dollars for her son Johnny's death. I received a check for one million dollars for my missing leg.

Well I'm so happy for you both that is great news.

Thanks Tim

It didn't hit Mrs. White yet maybe after the service is over.

Thanks GOD that our attorneys found the missing evidence that was held back from the trial. You should had seen Judge Baily he was ripen yelling at his attorney David Jackson and fired him in the courtroom after the jury read the verdict.

Mrs. White and I were yelling and jumping for joy. We were so happy then Bailey's attorney, Jackson just gave us a dirty look.

I have to go I will see you at the service.

Ok Linda thanks again for my phone.

I had finally finished cleaning up my place; I headed out to work to see Joey.

CHAPTER THIRTEEN

DON'T TRASH MY TRUCK

I arrived at work 3:30 that afternoon. I went through the garage said hello to everyone and headed upstairs to see Joey.

Hey Tim how are you doing?

I'm hanging in there Margaret.

Tim I'm sorry to hear about Mr. White.

Thank you.

Tim, what time does the service starts?

7:30 pm at O'Leary funeral home in Wethersfield. I will see you tonight.

Oh Tim if there is anything I can do? I would love to help you.

Thanks Margaret that's nice of you. I'm all set.

Ok let me call Joey to see if he's out of the meeting.

Joey, I have Tim here to see you.

Ok, I will send him to you.

Go ahead Tim, Joey is waiting for you in his office.

Thank you.

Knock Knock, Come in Tim have a seat son. How the hell are you?

I'm doing ok Joey. I'm sorry I've been missing work. I didn't kill anyone but I am happy he is dead! He and Ron Fisher had raped and brutally killed my mother. He got what was coming to him. I hope they catch up to Ron he is next.

Tim I'm so sorry for the bullshit you're going through son. Let me help you out, I have one of the best attorney in this state, David Jackson.

Tim asked Victor about David I hired him to get Victor out of prison, that man is great! I will hire him for you. I will call him right now, and then he grabbed the phone.

Joey that's nice of you. I thank you, but I'm all set I already have an attorney.

Well if you change your mind the offer is there. Next Joey put his left hand in his pants pocket. He pulled out a wad of cash, he started counting it loud as he hand me $800.00 dollars. Tim this is for you I know you can use it and you don't need to pay me back. The money is a gift for you.

No, Joey I can't take the money.

Please don't refuse me son! I want you to go and buy a new suit some shirts, ties, and dress shoes for court. Son you know what they say dress to impress it works all the time trust me.

Okay thank you so much. Tim go downtown on State Street and go into Luke's men's shop. That's where we buy our clothes. Ask for Luke, tell him you work for me and I sent you there. He will hook you up. Luke is a great friend and a good long time customer of mine. You know son I won't bring this up again anymore, but I have to tell you I will never forget to the day I die, how you were honest and looking out for my company, especially when you stood up to those a—hole and told them all, no more stealing you're not putting up with that crap and you fought for my company.

Tim no one does that unless your family, which you are now in our family. You're like a son to me. I have always taught my kids the same way honesty is the best policy. When you could have did like those other guys make your own route, but you chose not to thanks Tim. All of a sudden a loud voice came through the phones intercom yelling out Joey.

Excuse me Tim.

Go ahead Margaret.

Mr. Kid from Browns Spirit store is on line two. He said his trash container is gone and his fence is damage badly.

Margaret do you have his account in front of you?

Yes I do.

What are his balances on his account?

Zero he is paid up all the time never late, he is a great customer. Ten years he has been with us.

Margaret, how many yards was his can?

8 yards Joey.

Ok, I will talk to him now. Thank you.

As the speaker stayed on I was listening to Joey's conversation loud and clear. Hello Mr. Kid how are you sir? My name is Joey Marzano. Mr. Kid I'm sorry about what had happen I will send another can over your way and repair your fence.

Okay Mr. Marzano. Thank you.

Mr. Kid, you can call me Joey.

Ok Joey.

Who took my can may I ask?

I don't know sir. But I will find it. I'm sorry for this inconvenience. I will have a new can for you in about two hours.

Okay thank you have a nice day.

Oh one more thing Mr. Kid you won't be billed for next month's pickup. It's on the house or in this case it's on the can. Then Joey laughed

Then I heard Mr. Kid laughing hard. I like your sense of humor Joey that was good. Thank you Joey, that is nice of you.

You have a nice day.

You, too Mr. Kid thank you goodbye.

Margaret tell Bruce to fix the fence, and drop off a new 8 yard can, not a used can one over to Mr. Kid's store. I don't care if he has to work over time. I want that can delivered now!

Joey, we have a problem.

What's that Margaret?

Nicky, fired Bruce Monday.

Tell Russ to make the delivery and fix the fence.

Joey, you know Russ is not a fence repair man.

Yes Margaret.

But Russ should have no problem fixing that fence, he is a freaking welder.

Margaret, I'm getting tired of catering to these workers.

Tell Russ I don't care how he fixes that fence. I want it fixed today or he can find another job.

Yes Joey.

Then you need to call Bruce up, tell him that I said for him to get his ass back here tomorrow morning at 7:00am I will take care of him.

Joey, I don't know if Bruce will come back.

Margaret, why is that?

Well Bruce and Nicky got in a serious yelling match right before Bruce slammed the door on Nicky's face.

He told Nicky to go to hell.

Ha! ha! Nice I can't believe Bruce has a pair of brass balls.

Joey please be nice.

Sweetheart I am.

If Bruce gives you a hard time coming back, tell him I will give him an extra week paid vacation tell him this is between me, you and him no one else will know.

Hey Joey what about me?

Margaret, you know I take care of you all the time.

Did you enjoy Jerry Jones concert last week?

Yes, Joey thank you it was a great concert.

Oh one more thing I'm heading out for a meeting with a few investors they liked my invention, making electric with trash. Hopefully I can sell it for the right price.

Margaret, call up one of our account Sally's Bakery order a large fruit cake for Mr. Kid. Please tell Sally that I want fresh fruit on it.

I want the cake to be decorated with one of our new trucks front end loader, lifting up a can with the company name on the side of the truck. I'm going to take a photo of one of our new truck doing that. Then I will text her the photo.

Dam Joey, you're getting good with that Y-Phone.

I bought my grandson Garrett a Y-Pod so we can stay in touch with each other with that app we have it's called OUR-TIME we get to see each other as we talk with video chat.

Dam Joey your spoiling that boy.

I just love that boy.

You know Margaret I always say life is too short. Death is longer. Enjoy family while you can.

Oh Margaret Please tell Sally don't break the mold of the cake, we will be ordering more cakes throughout the year. Tell her to send me a text photo of the cake when it's done. And please tell her to deliver the cake to Mr. Kids address. I will pay her extra for whatever it will cost to make that delivery.

Yes Joey.

Thank You.

Tim I'm sorry I got to go.

Joey what do you think happened to the can?

I'm not sure Tim. I think it's a company trying to take over my territory. There is going to be another war. Just like it was in the Bronx.

Tim, take rest of the week off with pay. I will see you on Monday. I'm taking you off the truck for now. I will be putting you in the office in the sales department.

You are going to need time to get ready for court I understand. I thought if you're on the truck you won't be able to get ready for court. You have my permission to make your personal calls or meet with people just don't forget to sign up new customers. Your new hours will be 9-5 M-F. I may need you once in a while to fill in on a route on a Saturday giving Victor or Mackie a break.

Sure Joey, that sounds good thank you.

Joey, Joey what now Margaret?

Mackey is on the phone line two.

Margaret please tell Mackie that I'm in a meeting.

Joey I tried he said it's important he needs to talk to you, right now.

Ok it better be.

Put him through.

I will be right with you Tim.

Ok then Joey put Mackie on speaker phone. Mackey I'm in a meeting so what the hell is so important?

Yo, Joey.

The truck is on fire, flames are shooting out along with smoke coming out from the back of the truck.

What the hell is going on?

You better save my new truck! Your ass will be grass if not! I still owe 140 thousand dollars on that truck! Drive the truck to an empty lot open up the hopper, dump the burning trash out, and move the truck away from the fire don't get burned. As Joey was talking to Mackey he grabbed his cell phone and started playing with it. Then he asked Mackie are you at 500 block on Garden Street.

Yo, Joey how the hell did you know that?

I know where you guys are all the time, even where you should not be.

Keep on going down Garden Street take the first right on to Rose Terrace, there's an empty lot on your first left side, dump the truck there. I'm going to call the fire department now.

Ok Joey.

Mackey, I'm leaving the office now, I will see you on Garden Street bye.

Tim I will see you tonight.

Ok Joey, thanks again.

Margaret, call Bill Clark and reschedule today's meeting for Friday at the same time. Tell him I have an emergency to take care of and I'm sorry for cancelling.

Ok Joey, you got it.

Then a loud voice came through the speaker. Margaret I need to see you in my office now. Ok, Nicky I will be right there.

Margaret what is wrong?

Nothing, that I'm aware of Joey.

Margaret If Nicky gives you any crap you let me know when I come back. I will have a talk with him. Don't worry I have you covered.

CHAPTER FOURTEEN

MEMORIES

The funeral was hard to take. I was still in shocked and could not believe Mr. White was gone. My heart went out to Mrs. White the tears kept flowing as she walked over to the casket shaking Mr. White dead body hard. Yelling out loud, honey wake up, wake up, I love you and I want you here with me don't leave me please. The room suddenly became dead silent. Linda walked over to Mrs. White took her hand and walked her back to her seat and started talking to her to calm her down, then they both started crying.

To my surprise Duke, Tiny and Rusty are here attending the service, they all looked good, short haircuts no jeans or leather they were in suits. I almost did not recognize them. These three guys stayed at the White's house many times over the years when they came in town to see me. They are no strangers to the Whites they were family.

Mr. White favorite person was Duke. Mr. White enjoyed talking to him the most. He loved to hear Dukes stories about the club. He was so impressed with Duke. This one story really had touched him. He would always ask me many different times in his life to tell him about the time Duke and I and the club members went over to Saint Teresa Cancer Hospital for kids. All the kids that were able to walk, came outside and rode on the back of each bike. They took them around the block a few times.

All the children were so happy and excited. It really brought their spirits up. Especially when the kid knew they don't have much time to live. The hospital staff asked Duke if they could come back again and take the kids for a ride again. So Duke and the club member once a month continued their ride with the kids. Then the club did a charity run for the kids they raised enough money to buy Y-Pad's for each of the kids. That was a big hit the kids were so impress.

I remember that day Duke picked me up early from school. He was going to take me to the dentist, which was on the other side of town too far for me to walk. But first I went with Duke to the hospital for a meeting he had to attend. I waited in the hallway doing my homework. An hour later Duke got out of a meeting we both started walking and talking about getting something to eat, we were headed for the elevator when a lady yelled out excuse me Sir.

Yes Miss.

Are you Duke?

Yes how can I help you?

My name is Nancy Johnson.

Nice to meet you

Is this your son? Yes, I call him my adopted son Tim Ripple.

It's nice to meet you Tim.

Same, here Mrs.Johnson.

Duke my son Sam always talks about you all the time. You're his idol he loves you and your member's. I would like to thank you guys for taking out your time and enjoying the kids. They love to spend time with you guys and they love those beautiful bikes you guys really make their day. I just can thank you enough.

You're, welcome Mrs. Johnson.

Sam is a great kid.

Duke I'm a single parent, my husband was killed in Afghanistan last year. I'm so happy to see Sam has a male friend like you. Then she started crying. I was told today just a little while ago by Sam's Dr. Denton, that my son only has two weeks left to live. The cancer is starting to spread through his body fast.

I'm sorry to hear that.

Can you help me?

Sure what do you need?

Well Sam keeps on asking me if I could get him a leather vest like yours, with the letters and the Desert Kings Emblem on the back of the vest. That's his wish. Whatever the vest cost I will pay you back. I know you have to earn your colors.

No problem Nancy I will get the vest with the colors on it just like ours and we will take care of the cost.

What side jacket does Sam takes?

He takes a medium.

Nancy we all know about war, me and the guys were over there it sucks

Duke, Thank you so much.

Nancy is there a way I can get hold of you? I should have the vest next week.

Sure call me anytime then she handed Duke her business card.

Duke started to read it out loud Judge Nancy Johnson. Thank you Judge.

Duke please call me Nancy and don't hesitate to ask me if there is anything I can do for you or the guys just let me know.

Ok Thank you I will talk to you next week.

Little Sam never took off his vest even when Nancy took him out of hospital into the town for some ice cream. He even slept in it. He just loved it so much. Five weeks later Sam had passed away. The Judge buried Sam with his vest on. I was there with Duke and the all the members attended Sam's funeral and helped out with the service. There were twenty-three members that lead the service on their bikes, from the church to the burial site. So many people attended the service. There were a lot of bad talk going on from the streets, to the courthouse and law offices. Especially from the people that attended the services. Duke and four of the members were carrying the caskets into the church. People were shocked and upset speaking out saying how can the Judge associate with the Desert Kings? But the Judge did not care Duke and the guys were there for her and her son.

Everyone was surprised the next morning the local newspaper had a front page article about the Judges son funeral service. There with a few nice photos of the club members carrying the casket and leaving the church on their bikes. The other photo the newspaper had printed was Judge Nancy holding and squeezing Duke crying hard on his shoulder at the church. You can see tears rolling down her face as you saw the back of Duke wearing his colors Desert kings.

A week later Judge Nancy had sent a eighty two pound hog to the clubhouse, The guys roasted the hog on that Friday then the party started the next day. They had three kegs of beer. Teds band,{ The Up Beats} played all weekend. Duke even call Mrs. Carter the day before the party invited her to the party. She was thrilled, brought two trays of brownies she had made. Tiny picked her up. It was so good to see her laughing talking she even had a beer with Duke.

I took turns switching off with one of the band member Billy who was the lead guitarist while he was on the ground, mingling with the crowd and pounding down the beers. I was up on the stage playing my guitar covering for him jamming with the band.

The Judge was there with two of her close friend's. Duke invited his friends and neighbors. They all came with a dish they made, what a great time. Officer Davis was there dancing away with his girlfriend. There was so much food, Duke had called two of the food pantry in town, invited all the people to the party and they came and chow down. There were so many people at the party that the boys blocked off the street.

As time went on, Duke was staying in touch with Judge Nancy to make sure she was doing ok. Her and Duke became great friend and started dating Mr. White would always tell me how he could not believe how the club member's was so helpful.

He first was like other people always thought the club members were always in trouble. He had so much respect for the members after hearing this story from Duke.

As I was heading to the door to go outside to get some fresh air I had bumped into big bad cold hearted Nicky, to my surprised he was extremely polite as he had greeted me. As I continue walking down the stairs I heard a loud voice.

Tim.

Hey, Professor James.

Tim I'm sorry about Mr. White.

Thank you.

Let's go in I will introduce you to Mrs. White and Duke and the guys.

After the service was over, we all met at Carl Italian restaurant on the Berlin Turnpike in Newington. Between family and friends there had to be about 85 people.

We all had a great time everyone got to meet and talk to Duke, Tiny and Rusty.

Judge Nancy was going to come with Duke to Mr. White's service but she has a big trial going on and could not leave. But Duke said that she was coming to my trial. I just came back inside when I heard Linda and Mrs. White were asking Duke what I was like growing up.

Duke started telling everyone at the table stories about me, he was laughing so hard, before you knew it everyone there were laughing and smiling at me.

I could just imagine which story he was telling them. If I was to guess I would have to say how we met. I know it was not the story how he and the guys took care of Mr. Carter for me.!Ha ha!

Linda's eyes were glued on Duke. She always had a crush on him for years it was so obvious. Mr. White would love to joke with Linda about Duke she would laugh and her face would become bright red, she was a good sport. I could tell Linda's boyfriend that was sitting next to her was mad,by his facial expression that boy was pissed and jealous of Duke. It was good that everyone was having a great time, that's how Mr. White would have wanted it this way. As the waiter was filling our water glasses Joey called him over as he spoke to him in Italian?

A few minutes later the waiter handed Joey the bill.

Mrs. White came running over I will pay that bill.

Joey said please let me I had wish I had meet your husband I felt like I know him Tim always spoke highly of him he was a good man .

I would appreciate if you let me take care of this bill, that's at least I can do.

Mrs. White hugged Joey and started to cry Thank you so much Joey.

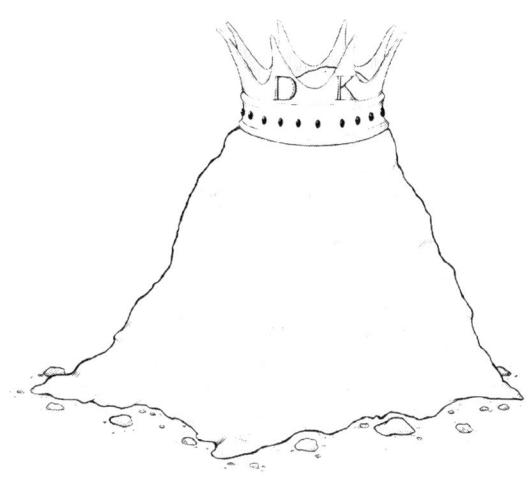

CHAPTER FIFTEEN

GOOD TIMES

W eeks had passed by it's been tough working in the office. I'm not use to being cooped up in one place. Man I really miss working outside.

Especially being on a truck where no one bothering me. Breathing that nice fresh air and the sun beating down on me. I really miss those great times with Victor and Katie, having fun joking, laughing, listening to that loud music. I miss the game battering up the rats. I miss the great views of those beautiful women walking around, shopping downtown Hartford. The different fragrance of women's perfume floating in the air as they were walking by us, those were the days. I would sometimes laugh out loud in the office, thinking about fun times Victor and I had. Sometimes I would get dirty looks from a few workers, but I didn't care. It was worth that loud laugh. I can remember Victor and me would take a break, getting some coffee and hang out on Pearl Street downtown.

I was shocked to see that so many women still had recognized Victor the champ. Women would come up to Victor smiling and ask him if they could have a photo taken with him. I would be snapping the photo with their phones. Man those girls loved it. Victor received so many phone numbers it was unbelievable. This was before Tammy was around I'm sure Victor is not like that anymore.!Ha ha!

One day I was taking a photo of Victor and these young girls, when a big black Cadillac stopped in front of us blocking my view of the shot. As they roll down the tinted window a voice yelled boys is everything ok?

Yes Sir.

Well, then let's get back to work.

Yes sir, it was Joey. As Joey left the girls would ask us who the man that was in that car. Victor always has some bullshit stories. His favorite line was oh that's my agent. I have to go to the gym now work out get ready for the next fight in Japan next week. It was nice talking to you lady's see you soon. That boy had an answer for everything.

I miss the overtime pay I use to get. I still can remember the times when I would come in early from doing my route one or two days a week at 5pm after working 12 hours instead of working in

14 hours those days. I was looking forward to go home and crack open a cold beer and relax.

Just as I was getting into my car in the work parking lot going home my cell phone was ringing it was a text from Joey Tim come in my office now please $$$.

Something about texting Joey was like a young kid he just loves to text. His newest trend was sending a voice message. He just loved that Y-Phone. I know what he wanted. When I see $$$ for sure I was right.

Once again big bad Mackey and his crew were up to their tricks skipping the banks afternoon pickup and leaving the job early. Mackie loved to hang out on the corner of Barbra and Rose Street with the boy's drinking and shooting dice. Joey wanted me to go and pick up the bank this was one of his biggest account he had and is about to lose it. He would pay me cash with a fifty dollar bill right out of his pocket as he handed it to me and thanked me once again for saving the banks account. I had also stayed on the clock to get more over time. When I came back to the yard I was leaving the office heading home I would hear Joey yelled out to Margaret to order another cake, sent it to Art Jennings at the bank.

I could not wait for my trial I hate the way people were staring at in the office and out in public, no matter where I' am people would make loud comment like, there the Mississippi killer. I tried not to let this bother me that is easier said than done. You get to know fast who are your real friends are in life.

This new office job Joey gave me was different and hard. I was on the phone trying to get new customers.

Sometimes the sooner I was to close the deal and was ready to go to meet the new customers to sign the contract, within minutes they would call me back and cancel our appointment.

It took me a while to realize what was happening. The people on the phone I was with had heard the news and remember my name. Tim, Joey is on line one for you. He said its really important.

Thank you, Margaret.

Hello

Tim I'm going to send you this text photo you need to see. I'm here at the grocery store buying lunch for the office. I walked over to the cooler to get some ice tea. I notice in the front of me is a half-gallon of milk, with your name and photo underneath big letters WANTED FOR MURDER and a phone number to contact the F B I .

No, way Joey.

Yes I'm not bullshitting you Tim. I just bought their last 25 half gallon of milk in the store so people won't see you. I hope the office likes milk. Maybe I will buy some chocolate syrup. Then he started laughing.

Thanks Joey.

Tim you need to use reverse psychology most time it works. Call the milk company now. Find out who is the owner of printing company. Tell the owner to stop printing your information now. Mention to him if he doesn't cooperate, you are going to sue him and take his company over. Then after you get his printing company you will put his name, photo on the front and back carton, of the entire milk carton thanking him for giving you his company, and for money he will have to pay you from winning the lawsuit. Tell the owner you will also put the same message on all the billboards on highway 91 both ways south and north from Hartford to New Haven. Tim, I have to go one of the milk cartons is leaking badly. I will see you soon in the office.

Ok, thanks Joey.

No problem Tim.

So I took Joey's advice and I called the printing company. I was able to talk to the owner Mr. Page nicely asking him to please stop printing my information on the milk cartons, but he just gave me a rash of crap. Then he started laughing and hung up on me.

Joey is pissed he called his lawyer David Jackson but he could no take my case he was too busy. Then Joey called Tony's lawyer, Pat Cole explained to him what was going on.

So, Attorneys Cole went down to the court house and file a civil law suit against Mr. Page who is the owner of the printing company. Then Attorney Cole had delivered the papers personally to Mr. Paul Page he did stopped printing my information on the milk carton, but it was too late the damage was done. Little did he knew he was about to lose his business.

People remembering the news when they heard my name or see my photo in any articles in the paper,and now on milk cartons. This bad publicity was killing me at work. I had a hard time signing up new customers.

Other workers had no problem they were sighing up contracts left and right.

Most trash companies would need a check from the new customer at the time of contract.

Joey was very creative he came up with great plan for new customers. No money down when the customer was signing the contract. He would collect two different credit card numbers and put them on the paper work. And use only one card in case they default payment. Joey would bill the new customer a month later.

The other smart idea Joey had is the people would sign a two year contract locked in the monthly payment would never go up even if dump fees or fuel cost did. New business was flowing in the office like crazy.

The six other surrounding garbage companies would get from the new customer the first and last monthly payment up front when the customers sign the contract. They all were pissed at Joey because they were losing business and lots of money. Joey did not give a crap. Four out of the six trash companies are related to him. They were Joey's brothers in laws, cousins, and 2nd cousin they all moved here from the Bronx. They all used to get along like one happy family but according to Joey the last five years they were constantly fighting over territory pricing and business.

Taking calls after a while I was able to recognize the voices of the other garbage company's Joey's family asking to speak to Joey. No one would ask for Nicky, nobody in the family member liked him. I had to be creative I had to change my name at work to Allan Grace. I told everyone the in the office what was happening in case a customer calls the office looking to speak to me. I worked out a deal with the Amy Jones the office manager. I would book the appointments and she would meet with the people, and get the contract signed. If the new customers saw me they would back out of the contract in a heartbeat. It worked out good Amy is a sweetheart.

According to Victor that Amy and Tony dated four years as she went to college and got a degree in business. Tony dropped out of college and decided to stay around to learn the family business. He broke up with Amy as she was finishing school. He started to date Constance whom is his wife now. The breakup was so hard for Amy. She was still in love with Tony. She started to drink heavy and was popping pills trying to commit suicide. She admitted herself to rehab after her graduation.

When Joey heard about her disaster he took it bad. He went to visit her, bought her a new yellow mustang her favorite color and had it delivered to the rehab. That was her graduation present along with her a job as the office manager. Boy that really pissed off a lot of workers Joey just loved Amy like his daughter.

Amy's father was a drug addict involved in two murders serving a lifetime sentence in Rikers Prison.

From birth, she never knew who her father is. Her mother always kept her from knowing the truth about her father, until Amy was older then she found out. She didn't want anything to do with her father. Joey has a kind heart when holidays came around he would buy groceries for her family.

Victor also told me he heard a rumor many times in the Bronx when he was there boxing, Joey knows a lot of people that Victor was friends with. Joey knows both Amy's mother and father when he ran his trash company in the Bronx after her father went to the slammer. Joey and Amy's mother had affair for years.

Amy has a brother Dominic, who is six year younger than Joey's son Tony. Joey also takes care of Dominic, he works part time for Joey as he is finishing college which Joey paid for.

Joey came to Connecticut to open his new trash company because he was paid off and was told to leave by the mob as they took over his company. Nicky just got out of prison serving ten years for murder. He had a lot of money so he bought in to Joeys new trash company.

They say Joey and Nicky are still associated with the mob.

After a few years in Connecticut Joey's trash business was doing good, Joey decided to move Amy's mother and the kids here to CT to watch and help them out. Joey does not know that Victor is aware of his affair he had with Amy's mother and about his son Dominic, otherwise Victor still could be in prison now.

Chapter Sixteen

Respect

The next morning I was in the office on the phone with Duke, he just got back from Mississippi. I was going over what he had found out about my case, when a loud voice yelled.

Tim, I want to know who is driving truck number 35, Victor or Mackie?

Sue hold on I'm on the phone.

Excuse me Sue don't you see that Tim is on the phone! Can you wait till he is off?

No I can't Amy you need to mind your own businesses Sue told her.

With all the noise going on I could hardly hear Duke so I told him I will call him back.

Sue and Amy were yelling and cursing at each other so loud that Joey came running into the office and started screaming what the hell is all the yelling about?

Then Amy told Joey.

Sue what's that call you had received Joey had ask her?

Well, Joey Miss Nickels said her brother Phil is blind, she was watching him from the house window walking to the bus stop on the corner of Franklin street and Jordan lane.

She had left the living room to go to the ladies room, a few minutes' later she came back and looked out the window to check up on her brother, she saw a man putting her blind brother into the garbage truck and driving away kidnaping him.

Margaret call Victor now!

Okay Joey here he is on the speaker phone.

Victor, what the hell is going on? And who the hell is your passenger you kidnaped?

Boss let me explain.

It better be good. You should know from the last time I caught your girlfriend riding around with you. Insurance won't cover passengers in case of an accident.

I had explained this to you before.

H E L L O! Joey hear me out first! Before you start laying your bullshit on me.

This better be good Victor!

I looked at Joey he is mad. Veins are popping out from his forehead, Go ahead speak-I'm all ears and listening, Joey told Victor.

Well I was driving down Franklin Street I saw this man lost his balance, he was trying to walk over a curb, and he slipped on some ice and fell flat on his face into the street. His red walking stick went flying across the street in the south bound lane when a truck ran over it and crushed it the man is blind. Cars just kept on going around him no one would stop to help this man. I could not just leave that poor Dude there. I took off my shirt wiped his head and face that was full of blood. I put the shirt around his head tied it with a little pressure. I was able to stop the bleeding in the meantime I was freezing my ass off.

Next I picked him up and lifted him into the truck then drove right to the hospital with the four ways emergency lights on. When I pulled into the hospital, emergency lane and started blowing the horn. I got crazy looks because of the truck but I don't care, I want to save the man's life. Some idiot came outside started yelling at me to move the truck out of the emergency lane instead of helping me with the man in the truck. I told him to shut his face or he will be sharing the same room with this poor guy is going in when I get through with him.

He is the one that probably call the office. That ass — -.

Victor you're not pissing on my back and telling me it's raining?

No Joey I'm not!

I know right then the crap was going to hit the fan. I knew that Victor been pissed at Joey for a while now.

Is Tammy with you? Is she on the back of the truck Joey asked Victor?

No sir.

Victor where the hell is she?

I told her to get some coffee for us! So she walked over to the coffee shop while I took this guy here. I will call her when I'm heading back to pick her up.

Victor why didn't you call the police? They would have taken in care of that man. Look how much of my time and money you wasted.

Joey, there is more to life than money. By the time the cops came here the blind man could die from bleeding to death or ran over in the street. The hospital is only two blocks away from there so I did the right move.

In who's opinion Victor, yours?

You know, Joey I just saved a man's life. You should be thanking me telling me I did a great job. Not chewing my ass out. I'm getting tired of you treating me this way. When are you going to stop? You never believe anything I tell you.

It's like you want me to screw up again so you will have an excuse to send me back to prison. I paid my dues in life. I've had cleaned up my act it seems like you have not notice.

I'm a different person than before.

We all are not perfect so give me a little respect like Aretha's Franklin said R E S P E CT. Not only did Victor spell the song out to Joey, but he put the phone next to the radio speaker and turned up the volume.

What a coincidence! The same song just came on the radio with Aretha singing her song RESPECT. The people in the office were trying not to laugh but it was hard not to.

The timing for the song to play was so perfect. That was like one out of a million times that could ever happen again. They say timing is everything. Boy they got that right.

Oh my God Joey was more pissed pounding the desk with his fist. He picked up a bunch of files on Sues desk and threw them across the room yelling into the phone turn off that freaking music now! I'm going to pull every freaking radio out of all my trucks.

Victor you should be in West Hartford at Beacon Hill Convalescent home! You should have been done with Hartford route two hours ago.

Joey these freaking roads are too icy! I cannot drive fast.

The conversation is getting louder and louder Joey is screaming from the top of his lungs into speaker phone. Everyone in this office was listening instead of working, even the office workers across the hall came in to hear what all the commotion that was going on here.

Then Joey said wait a minute Victor you need to shut up you just listen to me now. Joey was getting more pissed he kept on yelling at Victor as he started to lost his voice, don't you ever talk to me like that again. There was silence then we heard a loud voice that was coming through the phone that wasn't Victor.

Excused me sir are you the driver of this truck? Yes, why are you asking?

Well I'm with channel 13 TV station covering the news. I want to talk to you about the man you brought here and saved his life.

Will I be on the news tonight? Victor asked the reporter?

Yes you will.

Cool Dude.

Yo, give me a few minutes, I'm on the phone with my boss then I will answer any questions you have for me.

Okay, Thank You.

Go ahead Joey.

Click!

Joey hung up.

Everyone go back to work now Joey yelled out.

What the hell is that boy smoking?

Margaret call the medical center, set up appointment for a drug and alcohol test for Victor this afternoon.

Joey.

What Margaret?

Joan from the medical center told me last time they can only do one test a day per person by law. Either a drug test or alcohol test which test do you want Victor to take?

Both, Joey yelled out!

Margaret, tell Joan that I said I want both test done. If she does not want to give Victor both test like I asked. I will take all my business over to the new Medical Center off Governor Street. I also want her to draw blood from Victor for his drug test no swab in the mouth that's bull crap. And if Victor refuses to take both tests, tell him he is going back to the slammer automatic.

Dam, Joey what your doing is against the law.

Margaret I don't care I will fight it in court! Swab testing has been proven to be sixty five percent accurate and the blood test is ninety eight percent accurate.

But Joey

Yes Margaret

We both know that Victor know more about this part of the law than we do.

He knows from his fighting days that he can only take one test per day not two.

Victor is not that stupid Joey.

Yes, so.

But he is not in the ring Joey.

Oh yes he is, with me and if his test shows up positive I will kick his ass back to the slammer he is through, I'm not playing around with him anymore. He knows better than to question me.

Tim, calls Tony tell him I need to see him now.

Yes Joey.

Margaret please call Russ the welder and tell him to stop welding that can he is working on and to come up here now.

Tony will drive Russ over there to switch off Victor so he can go to his tests

Russ is going to finish the route with Tammy.

Joey what now Margaret?

You know Russ is going to be pissed when he find out he is going to be throwing trash. If he bitches tell that pre Madonna I said I can always replace him, welders are a dime a dozen. I could call the warden and he will send me a welder in a heartbeat.

Got, you Joey.

Thank You, Margaret.

I want Victor in my office not tomorrow but today now. Joey screams out, and then he looks at Amy and Sue and said, I want to see both of you ladies in my office now. Yes Joey they replied.

Chapter Seventeen

Where is the Judge

Finally the day was here May 15, 2014 8:00 am one hour before the court starts. I'm standing on the last step of the courthouse freezing my buns off waiting for Professor James. Its 12 degrees, windy, and snowing like crazy.

Hey, Tim How are you holding up?

Hello, Mr. James.

I'm a little nervous.

That's normal we just have to go over a few very important things before we enter the court room.

Okay.

Let's take a walk across the street to that coffee house. I'm sure you will enjoy a hot coffee. You got that right. Tim let me tell you first what's happening and the facts you need to know. Then I will answer your entire question. I may forgotten something that I told you before so don't mind me if I repeat myself.

Yes sir. Tim here this Y-Pad is for you to use. Tim let's use the app called Y-Message. So if you have any question or information for me just send it. I will do the same please turn your phone off. Judge Jade will go bananas when she hears a ring in her court room.

Tim there is going to be a lot of negative talk about you, don't get mad just bear it. Let it go into one ear and out the other. Keep your chin up, never have a look of anger on your face. The prosecutors are going to try to have a field day with you in front of everyone. Remember not only are you watching the juror, witness and the prosecutors, but you are also being watched.

Yes sir.

Did you take your phone with you on vacation?

Yes. I did. I took a lot of neat photo with it. I had installed an app that tell the, time, date, place, and where the photo was taken.

Tim, that sounds good. I will need to check out the history on your phone later.

Sure.

How did you get around the town?

I took a bus, taxis or walked.

Did you rent a car?

No.

Tim, where did you stay?

At the River Side Hotel on King Street.

Did you stay at any other hotel on your visit? No I got a great rate for staying there for ten days.

Tim did you see any video camera in any part of the hotel? Maybe in the lounge or in the hallway.

No, none that I recall.

Tim is there anything that you can remember after the fight when you took the taxis to the hospital then to the hotel?

Do you have receipts?

Yes there all here in this manila envelope here you are.

Great thanks Tim.

Oh, one more thing, Tim please don't call me Professor James just call me Ron.

Okay, Ron.

If you have any questions ask me?

Yes Ron.

Ron do you know any information about Judge Jade?

Yes she is a fair Judge, but firm.

Okay let's go in.

Ron,one more thing is bothering me.

And what is that Tim?

I did argue and fought with Joe Hall, In fact, I broke his nose. His blood was on my hand and shirt.

I did not kill him. I watched him get up from the ground before I left. I wanted to kill that man so bad, for what he did to Mom. But I didn't kill him I didn't have it in me.

Ron, have you received Duke's fax last night?

Yes I did, Duke is good he did a background check on all the jurors and witness.

Tim we are going to win this case.

Let's go inside it's getting late. We don't want to pissed off Judge Jade.

The courtroom was packed, as if there was a big party going on wall to wall people.

It was even hard walking to our seats without bumping into people. I came across Joey and Tony and got a big hug from Amy.

Bam! Bam! Bam! order in this courtroom now. Please take your seats. Please be quiet in this courtroom.

The people in the courtroom mouths had dropped open, with a mean look on their faces that could kill. They were all wondering who this Judge is. Where is Judge Jade?

Ron was surprise. But I did notice that the other Attorney Jackson's face was red with a look that I can't describe he just kept staring at the Judge Bailey in a daze.

All the people were sitting down except for Attorney Jackson. He was the only one still standing.

The Judge kept on hitting the gavel hard as he kept yelling out stop talking, and take your seats. He kept staring at Attorney Jackson then the Judge yelled out Counselor Jackson will you please take your seat? You're holding up my court session.

One of Attorney's Jackson, associate grabbed his arm and kept saying to him sit down as he pulled Attorney Jackson arm down.

Good morning, everyone my name is Judge Bailey. I am filling in for Judge Jade I will be the Judge for this case number70231 Tim Ripper the accused assailant charged for the of murder of Joe Hall in the State of Mississippi.

State of Connecticut is working with the State of Mississippi for the deceased Joe Hall.

Then the Judge yelled out to the courtroom guard, Randy could you please approach the bench?

Yes, your Honor.

I need you to lock the left side door. There are too many people standing. The set of doors on the right please don't let any more people come in until some people leave this court room. Any witnesses let them in. They should all be in here now.

Yes your Honor.

Thank you, Randy.

Order in the court, Excuse me! You three men that just walked in maybe you're in the wrong court room.

Isn't this courtroom 305 your Honor, Duke had asked?

Yes it is.

May I ask you who are you are here for? Is it for the deceased Joe Hall?

No your Honor, were here for the accused Tim Ripper.

You three men need to take off your leather vests. You cannot wear them in my courtroom!

But, your Honor Duke replied.

You heard me. Bam! Bam!

Take your colors off now if you plan to stay for the trial.

Your Honor?

Yes sir, Speak your mind. I'm listening.

Your Honor, I feel like we are on trial here. We all served our country. Came back from fighting wars overseas and thank God we made it back alive. Some of us are missing fingers, toes, and still have bullets in us. Your Honor the name of our club is Desert Kings. Then Duke looked at Tiny and yelled out to him show the Judge your vest

Tiny turned around as Duke explained to the Judge what the different patches meant. The whole court room heads were turned around to the back of the courtroom watched and listen to Duke.

We three served together four tours overseas in Iraq, Iran, Afghanistan, many of our friends never made it back. We all use to take life for granted. But no more, every second counts. Life is too short and death is longer, we don't realize how lucky we were to make it back alive. We all changed for the good, when we came back from the war. We do a lot of charity work, especially for the poor kids with cancer that may not see tomorrow. So now that you know the history about us and our club your Honor, I ask you if we can please keep our colors on in your courtroom out of respect for us.

The people in the room kept on looking at Duke then turned around watching the Judge to hear his answer?

The courtroom was so quiet you could hear people talking in the next courtroom through the walls.

Randy walked over to the Judge bench. He just stood there looking at the Judge to see what the next order was.

Excuse me sir what is your name Judge Baily asked?

Duke Singer your Honor.

Well Duke. Yes, you guys may keep your colors on. I respect what you guys did for all of us fought for our country thank you.

The people in the courtroom clapped and cheered as the guys took their seats.

Bam! Bam!

Order in the court lets quite it down now. Let's get started it's getting late Judge Bailey yelled out!

All of a sudden there is a loud voice talking in the back row and a loud bursting of laughter. Excuse me ladies, the ones that is sitting in the six row, seats 3and 4 on the right side would you both stand up please.

Yes your Honor.

What is so funny ladies? Share the joke with all of us. We all could use a good laugh.

No it's ok, I don't think so Judge.

I'm sorry miss I cannot hear you.

Can you please speak up louder?

And both of you ladies please take off your sun glasses there is no sun here and these dam lights in this courtroom are not that bright at all. Well! Well! Well! If it isn't Mrs. White and Miss Star! So ladies tell us all what is so funny?

Well Sir.

Excuse me Mrs. White, in my courtroom I'm addressed as your Honor, outside of the courtroom is whatever you want to call me have a some respect.

Yes your Honor,Linda and I were just saying a few weeks ago we remember seeing you and Attorney Jackson is here in this same courtroom. In fact your Honor you were standing right over there where Attorney Jackson is sitting right now, and he is still in shock seeing you here, once again as he is staring at you now. Then Mrs White started laughing hard. Your Honor you were standing in front of Attorney Jackson yelling and cursing at him so loud, that everyone in the courtroom heard you. Because he lost your grandson case it was finally over after six years in and out of this court house. Then when you were through screaming you told him he was fired. We were just saying that you two will never be seen together especially in the same courthouse never mind in the same courtroom. I guess we were wrong then she started laughing once again.

Judge Baily its funny how's life is, you can never predict what can happen? Won't you agree Sir?

Oh I'm sorry I meant your Honor?

The Judge didn't answer her question. He just stared at her with a mean look, wondering where she is going with this conversation, and wondering when will Mrs. White shut up and sit down.

Mrs White continued talking. Yes, you and your family your Honor, put us Linda and I through hell. Even though we won the case, we still lost.

Winning the case will never bring my son back to me. Nor will it bring back Linda's leg.

There is not a day that goes by that I don't think of my son John. I miss him so much. You could see the tears running down her face, her makeup is ruined as she kept on talking and crying

If you're disrespectable, troublemaker, ruthless, inconsiderate, spoiled rotten grandson of yours, didn't get drunk and drove your daughter's car into my son car at 75 miles an hour that night instead of doing the speed limit 40. My son would be here today she screamed out. Linda grabbed Mrs White arm and sat her down and comforted her.

Are you finished Mrs. White?

Yes your Honor.

Bam! Bam! Let's take a fifteen minute break. Everyone before we start this case please be back in this court room by 9:45 sharp. If you go out of the courtroom you better be back on time. The doors will be locked, and I don't care who you are your out. You could tell the Judge was embarrassed. By the looked on Judge Baily's face, he is pissed and was stuttering, puzzled for words to say next.

The courtroom was so loud people talking to each other about what just happen with the Judge grandson. Juror five was telling Juror six how she felt so sorry for Mrs. White. I lost my son Tommy at the age of eight, two years ago. When he was playing basketball, he missed the ball and went after it. He ran across the road when a speeding car hit him and never stopped to see if my son was okay. Shortly my son was pronounced dead in the ambulance going to hospital. Then the poor lady started to cry.

Attorney Jackson was talking to his associate's Counselor Tyler they both were looking and pointing at Mrs. White she just smiled and waved at them, it made them both even madder.

If the jurors didn't know about Judge Bailys case with his grandson. I'm sure they all know now.

I turned around and looked at Mrs. White she gave me a thumbs up, and I smiled at her.

Judge Baily returned to the courtroom with a pissed off look on his fat face. Then Judge started yelling will this court please be quiet now, take your seats. Bam! Bam! Before we get started any of you Counselors have any questions?

Yes your Honor; state your full name for the records.

Rick Tyler I'm the representing prosecutor for the state of Mississippi and Joe Halls family. I will be working this case along with Attorney David Jackson who is also the prosecutor in this case working with me and he is appointed by the State of Connecticut.

Is this true Counselor Jackson?

Yes your Honor, he replied.

Would the defense Attorney for this case please stand.

Yes your Honor, good morning my name is Ron James. I will be representing Mr. Tim Ripple who is the accuser for this case.

Thank you, Counselor James.

Counselor Tyler, what is your question?

Your Honor I'm wondering if we can wait and start this trial when Judge Jade comes back.

Why is that Counselor Tyler?

Are you not prepared Counselor?

Is there one of you witness last minute can't make it?

No your Honor.

Did you just get a call? Is there a death in your family?

No your Honor.

Then for heaven sake what the hell is your reason?

Everyone in the courtroom eyes was glued to Counselor Tyler, waiting to hear his answer.

Your Honor I know there is bad blood between you and Counselor Jackson. I believe that this is a conflict of interest and that this case should wait until Judge Jade is back to start this trial.

Counselor James do you agree with Counselor Tyler?

No your Honor. I don't.

Counselor James, could you please tell me and the court why you disagree with Counselor Tyler.

Yes your Honor, Jury's witness and everyone that is here for this trial had to make personal plans to be here. Many of the witness are from out of state. It would not be fair to reschedule this trial. I say let the trial begin now your Honor.

Thank you, Counselor James.

You may take your seat.

I have to agree with you Counselor James. It would not be fair to all the people here in this courtroom if we reschedule this case.

Let me explain to you Counselor Tyler. Not that I have to by all means! I just want to clear the air in this courtroom about my grandson's case. I was not on the bench when my grandson trial went on. So I did not represent him, nor did I hire Counselor Jackson my daughter did. I did not pay Counselor Jackson with my money. My daughter had paid him, so that mean that there is no conflict of interest. Do I make myself clear Counselor Tyler?

Yes, your Honor.

Your Honor I have another question?

What now Counselor Tyler?

Well are we trying this case under the Mississippi jurisdiction?

No this case will be ruled under these laws since the trial is here in the State Connecticut Counselor. I don't know where the hell you got that wrong information from. Counselor Tyler please approach the bench. If you should ask me any crazy question, I will disbar you from this case and my courtroom. Do you hear me Counselor Tyler?

Yes your Honor.

Counselor James I did not receive your witness list can I make a copy of it?

Hear you are your Honor.

Thank you.

Please take your seats gentlemen.

Everyone please shut off your phones. I don't want to hear any phone ringing.

If I hear a phone ring I will take that phone from the party and they will never see that phone again. I will donate their phone to a great cause. Believe me I will take that phone. I have done this my times. Tablets are fine to use as long as there quite.

Mr. Ripple how do you plea young man?

Not guilty your Honor.

Thank you Mr. Ripple you may take your seat.

I will read out loud a list of witnesses if you hear your name please stand. If I didn't call your name, when I finished please raise your hand.

I would like all the witnesses to repeat after me. I swear to speak the truth and nothing but the truth so help me God. You all may take your seats thank you.

Judge Baily stood up turned his body facing the jury and said keep in mind that Mr. Ripple is on trial. Do not assume he is guilty. He deserved a fair trial like everyone else that appears in this court, so listen to the case you will determine the right honest answers thank you.

Counselor Jackson would you please call you first witness to the stand!

Thank you your Honor.

Calling Sergeant Kraft please take the stand.

Good morning Sergeant.

Good morning Counselor.

Sergeant how did you meet the accused Tim Ripple?

On January 3, 9:30 am 2014, Tim Ripple come in to the police station and introduced himself to me. Then he asked me if he could get a copy of his mother's brutal murder report. He asked me some questions.

And what type of questions?

Why, weren't the murderers *caught*?

I explain to Mr. Ripple we had worn out his mother case trying to find the killer. And we were told to move on to a new case. His mother case was cold and old. Mr. Ripple wanted to know when a case is considered a cold case. I told him in Mississippi it was to the day of the murder eight years is considered a cold case.

And how did Mr. Ripple react after you told him?

He was very upset and angry.

Any other questions that Mr. Ripple had asked you that you may remember?

Yes he was a little chocked up when he asked me if I know if his Mom was dead before the killers cut off her two toes.

According to the autopsy report, his mother was alive when the killers cut off her body parts. She was shot up and was overdose with a strong street drug called supper high which was in her system.

I also mention to Mr. Ripple, that the paper never said the killers also took his mother's middle finger of the left hand.

To this day his mom's body parts were never found. He had asked me if it was true if his mother was raped.

And what was your reply Sergeant Kraft?

Yes she was I told him.

When I told him, tears came down his face, and he asked me if the semen ever had been tested for DNA. Then Sergeant Kraft just stopped talking and glanced at me.

Continue, what is the result from the sperm test?

Then Sergeant Kraft said excuses me. Counselor Jackson his poor mother is dead lets her rest in peace.

You know how it works in court Sergeant Kraft.

May I remind you, you're under oath?

Objection your Honor I have to agree with Sergeant Kraft let's not drag this out, let's move on.

Objection, overruled Counselor James.

We want to hear the reason, continue Sergeant Kraft.

Yes your Honor.

The sperm was destroyed according to the DNA testing. Sergeant looked right at me, and said son I'm sorry to bring this up again.

Go ahead Sergeant, continue please. Yes your Honor.

How can that be?

Well at the time of the rape the victim had her menstrual cycle.

There was too much body acid between the blood, and the drugs. The drugs were not pure they were cut with some type of filler. Our labs to this day don't know what the drug dealers used for fillers to cut the drug. But whatever those fillers were in the drug ate up all the sperm and DNA that we were going to use for evidence.

Sergeant Kraft did the rapist wear a condom?

No, we did not find any.

Does this happen a lot where the body acid and drug destroys the evidence?

No, Counselor Jackson.

But we did see this happen one time before with a murder case I recall about five years ago.

Was there anything else Mr. Ripple asked you?

Yes, there is Counselor Jackson.

Tim asked about the ten thousand dollars that was in her pocketbook that was lying in the back seat if we still had it? I, asked the Chief about it, she said she didn't think the money was still the in the evidence room it's been too many years. But she said she would check it out. Then she will call Tim back either way.

When the case became a cold case and if no one claims the money, the police department will have given the money to charity?

The police department had put an ad in the newspaper, hoping that someone in his the family would come in and claim the money. No one ever did.

Which nobody would of found the money because it was hidden in his mother's blouse.

The blouse was in the bottom of the evidence box. The Chief, happen to lift the box and walk over to the table, the bottom of the box open up and everything fell to the floor. The chief was picking up the evidence of his mother from the floor. She noticed the money was in a clear plastic bag and fell out from the right side of the long sleeve blouse of Mrs. Ripple someone had taped the bag of money inside the sleeve and now over the years the tape had dried up .

The Chief called Tim late that afternoon, to let him know to her surprise she had found the money. Tim came in early the next morning and took his mother's money. He thanks me and the Chief.

Thank you, Sergeant Kraft

Counselor James, It's your turn to cross-exam.

Thank you.

Good morning, Sergeant Kraft.

Good morning, Counselor James.

What were some of the other question Mr. Ripple asked you?

If I was involved working on his mother case?

And what was your answer?

Yes, I just started at the Biloxi police department that week and his mother murder was my first case.

Continue Sergeant Kraft, well Tim asked me if Joe Hall was ever been brought in for questioning for his mother murder. I told him yes we did bring him in twice. We didn't have enough evidence to put him away. DNA back when his mother's murders took place was not quite as accurate like it is today. The murderers wore gloves and were very careful not to leave any evidence.

Objection your Honor.

This question and answer I would like to strike from this case file your Honor Sergeant Kraft is not on trial here.

Overturned Counselor Jackson, yes your Honor.

Continue Counselor James get to your point. I'm not wearing my dancing shoes and my feet are getting tired.

You can hear some of the people in the courtroom were laughing.

Yes you're Honor.

Two years later after the investigation was going on Joe Hall was picked up and convicted of robbing and raping and killing a young lady in her early twenties.

When the coroner did the autopsy on the young lady she was four months pregnant, the baby was dead.

Just as Sergeant Kraft finished talking there was a loud cry coming from a juror.

Mrs. Steel are you ok?

Yes your Honor.

I just received a text from Duke. Telling me about Mrs. Steel story and what she was about to tell the Judge. Then I turned around and gave Duke a smile. I'm sorry your Honor. I had a miscarriage last year due to a car accident. The doctor told me I could not conceive another child due to the accident.

Then the poor lady started crying like crazy as all the eyes in the courtroom is on her.

Mrs Steel, I'm so sorry to hear that.

Thank you, your Honor.

Bam! Bam! Judge Baily is pounding the gravel yelling out let's all take a fifteen minute break.

After break Judge had asked Mrs. Steel if she was ok.

Yes your Honor I am thank you.

Let's continue go ahead, Counselor James.

Sergeant Kraft, was Joe Hall ever question in prison about Mrs. Ripple murder?

Yes he was.

He would never admit he had killed her. Are you kidding me? If he did confess he would have been kept in prison longer.

Joe Hall would just laugh at my questions. Then he described what type of clothes she was wearing at the time of the murder, and beauty marks, and scars that were on Mrs. Ripple body. But we still had no concrete proof that he was the killer.

Objection your Honor, we need to move on.

Overruled,Counselor Jackson.

You may continue Counselor James.

Please continue Sergeant Kraft!

Joe Hall served nine years in Mississippi penitentiary. He was released last year.

I have no more questions at this time. You may take your seat Sergeant Kraft thank you.

Bam! Bam! Then the Judge said. It is late lets report back here tomorrow morning at 8:30am everyone have a nice evening.

Chapter Eighteen

Attitude
⟹

Good morning everyone.

Good morning Judge.

Counselor James, I believe you're up, please call your next witness to the stand.

Yes your Honor. Miss Pam Hayes to the stand please. Good morning Miss Hayes.

Good Morning, Counselor James.

Miss Hayes, I would like to thank you for being here today.

You are welcome James Counselor.

I would imagine it is colder in Hartford than it is in Biloxi.

Yes, it's not only colder, but there is more snow here we get very little in Biloxi.

Miss Hayes did you ever meet the accuser Tim Ripple?

Yes sir, I have.

Could you please point him out to the court?

He's in the first row, third seat, wearing a blue shirt and that sharp tie.

Thank you, could you please tell the court how you met Mr. Ripple?

Sure, I work at City Hall. It was January 3rd 2014 on a Wednesday at 8:10 am. Mr. Ripple walked in and I was passing him in the hallway, he had stopped me and asked me where the police station was located. I gave him a map of the city then I walked outside and showed Mr. Ripple how to get there. I told him it was cheaper to take a bus instead of the cab so he walked over to the bus stop and I went back to work.

Was there any talk of why Mr. Ripple was in town?

He just told me his mother was murder and he wanted to get the police report. I felt his pain when he looked at me and spoke in a low voice. I didn't want to ask him any more questions.

Thank you Miss Hayes. I have no further questions at this time. Counselor James sat down.

Counselor Jackson you're up Sir. The Judge announced.

Thank you, your Honor.

Miss Hayes, was there any other time that you saw or met with Mr. Tim Ripple?

Yes.

Could you please tell the court the details?

Well two days later, I was on the bus going home from work and a few stops later. Mr. Ripple got on the bus with that map I gave him. He was reading it as he was walking to get a seat not paying attention he tripped over someone's leg. Then he landed right on my lap. I asked him how it was going and he said it was a pleasure bumping into me again. Then I started to laugh so hard that people on the bus were laughing too. He looked up at me in shock, his face turned red and then he had apologized. I moved over a seat so he could sit down next to me then we talked.

Miss Hayes what were you two chatting about?

Objection your Honor, Miss Hayes is not on trial here.

You are right Counselor James, it is your client Mr. Ripple. Overrule, continue Counselor Jackson.

So what was your conversation about? He continued.

Small talk, like our jobs, family, friends and then Mr. Ripple asked me out for dinner that night.

Miss Hayes, where did you go for dinner?

I met up with him at 7:00pm at Biloxi Blues Café on Beach Boulevard. They have great food, I love their famous sea food burger and they have magnificent bands for entertainment.

Did you both have any cocktail?

Yes, why do you ask?

Well Miss Hayes, here is a man visiting your hometown, you don't know him from Adam. He could be a killer but yet you meet up with him, go out to dinner, and have cocktails with him etc. Don't you think that it's a peculiar behavior and not smart on your part? Do you do this a lot? Go out with guys you just met that day?

Objection your Honor.

Please strike this question from the file and let it be noted that Counselor Jackson is badgering my witness. He needs to keep his personal comments to himself.

Sustain, I have to agree with you Counselor James.

Yes Betty, could you please remove the last few questions from the report?

Yes your Honor.

Thank you

Counselor Jackson, the plank that you are walking on is getting shorter. You better start watching your steps.

Your Honor may I please speak?

Yes Miss Hayes, the floor is yours young lady.

Thank you. Excuse me, Counselor Jackson.

Yes Miss Hayes?

For the record, you are being very rude and insulting towards me. For your information Counselor Jackson I have a master degree in Human Behavior and a Bachelor's degree in Psychology, I can read people very well. From the time that I have been with Mr. Tim Ripple, I could tell he is a gentleman, kind, and a caring person. He has a very positive outlook and he knows what he wants in life. Tim Ripple is not a killer.

Mr. Jackson, speaking of reading people, I can tell that you hate the world. The way you speak, your tone of voice, the twitch in your left eye and your hands is shaking holding that report. You have probably just been through a bad divorce or relationship recently or maybe it's not over yet. Maybe you need a drink, you're going through withdrawals, besides other personal issues in your life you have. You should try to be nicer to the public, things can always be worse.

The people in the courtroom were clapping, cheering Miss Hayes on.

Thank you, your Honor, I'm all through.

You're welcome Miss Hayes.

Counselor Jackson started to walk back to his chair and stopped fast and turned around and looked at Miss Hayes as she is getting up from the witness stand.

Oh I'm sorry just one more question, Miss Hayes is your blood type rare, AB negative?

Yes, it is Counselor Jackson.

Thank you Miss Hayes.

Objection your Honor, that is relevant to this case what blood type my witness is?

Bam! Bam! Betty, please make sure you remove that last inconsiderate question Counselor Jackson just asked Miss Hayes.

Yes your Honor.

Thank you.

I need to see you three Counselors in my chambers now.

Bam! Bam! This court will adjourn, for one hour and a half and we will return here at 1:00 clock sharp to continue.

Tim I will meet you guys at Gardenia Street Café. I will be a little late. Okay could you please order me a burger and fries?

Sure Ron.

Hey Duke.

Hey, Tim man what a trial.

You got that right Duke.

Tim, are you doing okay?

Yes Duke.

Glad to hear it as he patted me on the back.

Guys I have to go and see the Judge. Counselor James said. I don't want to piss him off. I believe Counselor Jackson did a good job doing that.

The cloud is hanging over that boy now.

You got that right Tiny. Everyone was laughing.

Mrs. White you and Linda follow me, we all going to Gardenia Street Café for lunch.

Okay son, we will see you there.

Knock, Knock come in, Counselor James have a seat I will be off the phone in a minute.

The chamber was quite, Counselor Jackson and Counselor Tyler keeps on staring at the Judge as they were both listening to his phone conversation. The two were making strange faces at each other as they were listening to the Judge conversation. The Judge kept on arguing on the phone, his voice was getting louder and louder. Counselor Jackson left eye started to twitch like crazy, knowing that the person that was on the phone with the Judge was getting him prime up.

Okay bye then, the Judge slammed the phone down.

Counselor Jackson what the hell were you thinking, when you asked Miss Hayes what blood type she is?

I can explain your Honor.

It was all uncalled for.

But your Honor.

No if, ands, or butts or maybe for that matter Counselor Jackson, I don't want to hear it.

You will be sitting the trial out for a while Counselor Jackson. Counselor Tyler you will be taking the case over.

Counselor Jackson, when I feel that it's time for you take back the stand I will call you.

Do you have any question Sir?

No your Honor.

Does anyone have any question?

No your Honor.

Same here you're Honor.

Counselors are everyone's witness list up to date?

Look at the list again make sure it is correct and if there is someone not on the list tell me now I don't like surprises.

I'm good.

Same here.

Okay gentlemen lets go to lunch.

Chapter Nineteen

Mirror Never Lie

B am! Bam! Good afternoon everyone. Let's get started. Mr. Ralph Gray to the witness stand please.

Thank you Counselor James.

Your welcome your Honor .

Good afternoon Mr. Gray thank you for being here today. Your welcome Counselor James.

Mr. Gray do you own The Biloxi Blues Café on Highway 90 in Biloxi Mississippi?

Yes I do. Were you working on the evening of January 4 2014?

Yes, I was.

I served Mr. Ripple and Miss Hayes at the bar. Mr. Ripple had a scotch and soda with a twist of lemon. Miss Hayes had a slow orgasm against the wall.

Bam! Bam!

Mr. Gray we are not at your café please watch's your language.

Your Honor this is a name of a popular drink, Miss Hays orders it all the time.

All the people in the courtroom were laughing hard. Judge was even madder this time knowing he had stepped in a larger pile of crap.

Bam! Bam!

Then Judge Bailey started yelling out silence in my court room now.

Continue Mr. Gray I know Miss Hayes and her girlfriends they are regulars.

Miss Hayes has a hell of a arm she is the champ. I sponsored a dart team every year. This is the third year my team came in first place, not too many people can beat Miss Hayes although they tried hard, but she still holds the record.

Have you ever met the accused Mr. Tim Ripple before?

Yes, Counselor.

So tell the court what was Mr. Tim Ripple behavior like that night?

Sure, Counselor James.

Well to be honest with you he saved my life no pun intended. The courtroom was roaring with laughter.

Objection your Honor this is not a joking matter.

Overruled, Counselor Tyler.

Mr. Gray, youbetter have a good answer.

Yes, your Honor I do.

Counselor Tyler is right this is not a joking matter.

Yes, your Honor I know that. I was not trying to be funny it just came out that way.

I just got finished serving Tim and Pam drinks when Bobby from the band name (Two Blocks Down) is supposed to play that night came up to me, to tell me the bad news the lead guitar player Jimmy had a flat tire and had no spare tire with him. He is stuck in Louisiana is not going to make it tonight.

So Bobby tells me the band has to cancel. I was upset my café was packed, people came from all over to see this band play, and they're the number one band in the state.

I told Bobby no way you're going to kill my business if you don't play tonight.

So, what happen next Mr. Gray?

Mr. Ripple said to me. I don't mean to listen to your conversation sir, but you're right in front of me. Its sounds like you're in a jam.

I can help you.

Sir I can play a mean guitar. I can play any songs.

I'm good, I don't mean to brag, I just love to play.

I had asked him if he doesn't mind playing.

No not at all he said to me.

This will be a pleasure to play with this band.

I thanked him and told him I will pay him cash when he was done playing that night plus free dinner, all the drinks they wanted it's on the house for him and Miss Hayes.

I introduced Tim to Bobby and the band. Bobby told Tim that he could use Jimmy's guitar it was just tune up ready to play. Then the band jammed the house down all night long.

Let me tell you the customer had a great time dancing and singing along, business was great that night.

So Mr. Gray did you pay Tim?

I tried, I handed him one hundred fifty dollars.

Objection your Honor there is a conflict of interest Counselors Tyler yelled screamed out.

Sustained, no it's not your Honor.

Bam! Bam! Counselors would you both please approach the bench now.

Jury two was talking soft to jury three, he looked at her nod his head and smile.

Counselors, this is how it's going to work. Then Judge Bailey started to whisper. I still could hear him from where I was sitting.

If Mr. Ripple took the hundred fifty dollars then yes Mr. Gray will be removed from this case, conflict of interest.

If Tim didn't take the money then he can continue.

One more stipulation I am adding.

And what is that your Honor?

Well Counselor James if your witness Mr. Gray served Mr. Ripple, five drinks or more within three or four hours when he was there playing, Mr. Gray will be removed from the witness list conflict of interest once again.

Is there that any more questions gentlemen?

No your Honor.

Same here your Honor.

So Counselors lets continue.

Excuse me Mr. Gray for the interruption.

So Mr. Gray going back to your conservation, tell the court how many drinks did Tim Ripple consumed that night?

None

What do you mean none?

Mr. Ripple drank club soda with a wedge of lemon all night six of them to be exact.

Thank you.

Mr. Gray I have no more questions for you at this time.

Counselor Tyler,you may cross exam the witness.

Thank you, your Horror.

Good afternoon, Mr. Gray.

Good after noon Counselor Tyler.

Mr. Gray did Mr. Ripple take the $150.00 from you at the end of the night?

No Sir, he did not.

Do you mean Tim Ripple played for free that night?

Yes he would not take the money.

But he did ask me if I ever saw Joe Hall in my club as he showed a photo of him just released from prison two years ago.

Mr. Gray what was your reply?

Yes, he comes in usually on Friday night about seven. He sits at the bar and drinks five whiskey on the rock until about ten thirty when another guy comes in and has a drink with him then they would both leave. So what happen next Mr. Gray?

Bam! Bam! Mr. Tyler, remember what I told you.

Yes your Honor.

This is the last question I will ask.

Thank, you Counselor Tyler.

Mr. Ripple came back the next night at 8:00pm without Miss Hayes.

No further question at this time?

Bam! Bam! The court will adjourn until tomorrow. May I remind everyone including Mr. Ripple, from the juror, to the accuser, to all witnesses to all the counselor and prosecutor there will be no communication with each other outside of this courtroom until this case is over?

Any question?

Speak up now.

Bam! Bam! Court is adjourned until tomorrow morning at 8: 30 am Good night.

The night went by so fast I could of use more sleep. I was sitting in the courtroom trying to stay awake when I heard.

Bam! Bam!

Good morning everyone.

Good morning your Honor.

Take your seats everyone and let's get started now. Both of you Counselor's please approach the bench.

Thank you.

I'm sorry I meant all three of you please bring up your witness list.

Thank you,Counselors.

All of sudden a loud sound of a ringtone came from the middle of the courtroom. Bam! Bam! The Judge is hitting the gravel hard.

Officer, Will you please take that phone away from that lady now.

Yes, your Honor.

Thank you.

You know how I hate ringing cell phone in my courtroom!

Excuse me your Honor could I please have my phone back after court is over today?

Miss I'm sorry but I told everyone to shut off their phone in this courtroom.

Your Honor I was not here yesterday.

Miss why are you here today?

Your Honor,I work for a local newspaper. I'm filling in for the reporter that was here yesterday. I'm doing a story on this trial.

Miss could you please, stand up when you're talking to me. Show me a little respect, since you didn't happen to have it with your phone!

Yes your Honor.

Miss, do you wear glasses for reading?

No, your Honor.

That's too bad! People in the court room were smirking.

Excuse me your Honor!

Yes Miss!

You're Honor I don't understand. What does wearing glasses have to do with my phone?

A lot Miss, if you told me yes I do wear reading glasses and I had forgotten to bring them with me. Then I was going to give the phone back to you after court is over. I would understand you could not read the sign on the doors.

The rules for the courtroom reads, no eating, or drinking no phones or beepers on. Only tablets are aloud they must be on vibrate.

Maybe you were talking on the phone while you were walking through the doors! So you did not see the signs in front of you.

The people in the courtroom could not stop laughing.

Bam! Bam! As he slammed the gavel and yelled out quiet in this courtroom!

Miss the answer to your question is no. You can't have your phone back! Please have a seat I would like to get started now we are running late.

Counselor James why do you have a new witness on your list?

Doctor Jones could not attend court hearing before due to his schedule in the hospital your Honor.

And who is this Doctor Jones, Counselor?

Your Honor Doctor Jones is the one who was in the hospital and treated Mr. Ripple after he and Mr. Hall were in the brawl that night.

Counselor Jackson and Counselor Tyler would you both objected if Doctor Jones takes the stand? It's up too both of you.

No your Honor its fine he can take the stand. I'm speaking for both of us your Honor.

Thank you Counselor Tyler.

Okay gentleman, let's proceed. Counselor James, call up your next witness. Mr. Watson, to the stand please.

Good morning sir.

Good morning Counselor James.

Mr. Watson tell me, do you own a jewelry store across the street from the Biloxi Blue Café?

Yes sir.

I would imagine, you must have video cameras set up inside and outside of your store?

Yes I do.

Do you recall watching the video of the night of January 6'th of this year?

Yes sir, I watched it the next morning before I opened the store. Then I made a call to the police they came to my store that afternoon and asked me to take the digital chip.

So Mr. Watson, tell us what you saw on the video.

Well in the alley next to the café, there was an old man and a young man arguing, and all of a sudden hands were flying all over. The fight broke out. I could not hear the conversation the music was too loud.

Mr. Watson could you tell the court what else you've seen in the video.

The old man punched the young man in the face. The poor young man fell to the ground in pain. He got up slow started to staggered back and forth as he was walking, he looked like he was dizzy, and then the young man throw a fast punch at the old man who landed on the ground. The young man got on top of the old man and keep on punching him in the face yelling and cursing at him. Then to my surprise the old man pulled a big knife out from his boot and stabbed the young man twice in the left leg.

What happen next?

The young man had a hard time getting up from the ground but he did. He looked like he was in so much pain. He was screaming as he pulled the knife out of his leg then went hopping away with a trail of blood following him.

Continue please, Mr. Watson.

Well the old man wiped the blood off his face as he was getting up from the ground. Then he walked away.

So what happen to the knife? No one seems to know it's gone. Mr. Watson tell the court if you see any of those two guys that were fighting that night. Are they in this courtroom?

Yes, he is right there in the front it's the young man whose nose is bleeding now. Thank your Sir.

Bam! Bam! Mr. Ripple are you ok?

Yes your Honor.

Would, you like to go to the men's room?

Yes your Honor.

Thank you

I started walking fast to the back of the courtroom heading for the doors to get out. Fumbling with the doors they were locked. I kept on pulling the doors until the officer finally came over and unlocked it. As I was walking out of the courtroom, I heard the officer called a custodian on his radio telling him to come quickly and wipe the blood off the door handle, and mop up a puddle of blood that I left on the floor in the courtroom.

I was walking fast down the hallway looking for the men's room.

The blood from my nose was flowing out faster I couldn't stop it. As I walked faster I noticed a janitor wearing an oversize gray uniform and a red baseball cap he was bending over cleaning the water fountain.

Excuse me, I believed I had dripped blood all over the hallway floor. I'm sorry. Could you please mop the blood, so no one will fall.

Sure.

Thank you could you please tell me where is the men's room is?

Go straight ahead take the next left and the first door on the right.

Thank you.

The janitor never once turned around to look at me as I was talking to him. Instead he just continued to scrub the metal in the water fountain and admiring the shine. I walked in the men's room headed straight to the sink, I looked into the mirror took my suit jacket and tie off, hung them both on two stall door down from me. I took off my shirt, put some soap on the blood stains and scrubbed the stain out. I grabbed some paper towels from the dispenser and slid the clean trash can under the hand blower. I put the paper towels on top of the trash can and laid my shirt on the paper towels. I was thinking of a way that I could keep the hand blower on. I quickly took out a piece of gum from my pocket and started chewing it. Within a few minutes I took the gum out of my mouth and jam it in between the ON button on the hand blower that was hanging on the wall. I needed the blower to stay on to dry my shirt. I looked at my watch and noticed I've have been gone twenty one minutes already. I need to hurry up and get back in the courtroom before they come and get me.

Finally my nose had stopped bleeding. I started to wash off the dry blood from my face and neck. I was just about finish when I heard the bathroom door open. I was thinking it is the court officer coming for me. I heard a loud noise like someone was locking the bathroom door from inside. I bent my head over the sink and cupped my hands splashing the water in my face. I just glimpse quickly in the mirror had seen which was the back of the red hat just like the same hat the custodian had on.

I quickly walked over to the blower to check my shirt. Thank God it was dry. I pulled the chewing gum out from the dryer to stop it. I started to get dressed, walked over to the sink, and I could not help but to hear that there was a lot of loud noises coming from the stall where the janitor was in. I tried to grab my watch from the top of the sink when I slipped on the wet floor and knocked my watch off the sink. It hit the floor and had shattered. Dam it I yelled out forgetting that there is someone else is in this bathroom beside me.

Then the stall door slammed open. Are you ok Tim a voice yelled at me?

Yes I answer quickly. Who are you? Do I know you? There was no answer. I started to adjust my tie as I looked into the mirror and suddenly I froze.

I was looking at two of us with the same face. I'm in shocked, I started pinching my neck thinking maybe I'm dreaming, I didn't sleep good last night worrying about the trial.

Tim what you see is true. My name is Sue Ripper; I am your twin sister. Here touch my hand I'm real.

It's nice to meet you. How did you find me?

Tim your nose is bleeding.

So is your nose Sue!

Then there was pounding on the bathroom door. Tim Ripple are you in there? Open this door now!

Tim I really need to talk to you, we have so much to talk about. I will catch up with you later. I know how to get hold of you. Tim I got to get out of here now. I just heard the court officer pounding on the door looking for you. She keeps on talking as she slipped on the custodian uniform and tucked her hair under her red hat. Then she glued her fake mustache and grabbed her mop and walked out the door.

Tim are you ok?

Yes sir. I'm just finishing cleaning up.

Let's head back to the courtroom, the Judge is looking for you.

CHAPTER TWENTY

PARTY TIME

A few months had passed by my court case is still going on I been feeling stressed out trying to win my case. Thinking that the end is coming soon and it does not look good for me, I'm getting scared. I was at work on my cell phone talking to Duke when I heard through the intercom phone on my desk Joey is calling me. Once again I told Duke I will get back with him. Then I heard Joey say, Tim I need to see you right now in my office!

Yes Sir.

Yes please shut the door and have a seat.

Tim there is two things I want to ask you?

Sure Joey what's up?

Victor and Tammy want to take this Saturday off. Tammy is going to have her first fight in New Haven. Do you think that you can drive her route this Saturday?

Yes, but I ready need to pick up Peter. I've been trying to spend time with him on weekends, but my ex-wife is playing games with my scheduled visiting days with him. Finally I got him this weekend.

Tim you have my permission to pick up Peter at his house Saturday morning with my truck he can ride with you all day as you two can do Timmy's route. I don't care about the insurance policy about no riders.

Yes sure Joey I will work Saturday.

Thank you.

Joey pulled out a fifty dollars bill out of his pants pocket and said this is for you take this money you and Peter enjoy lunch on me.

Wow,thank you Joey that's so nice of you.

There is one more thing Tim.

Yes Sir.

I'm having a party this Sunday celebrating Tony's daughter Tina coming into the family. I'm inviting all of my family and friends over. I want you to come, if you have no plans. Peter is also welcome to come he can play with my grandkids.

We will be there.

Thanks Joey.

Saturday was fun Peter was having a blast riding around in the garbage truck.

We stopped at Peter's favorite hamburger restaurant for lunch. A few hours later I pulled the truck over and bought us an ice cream cone.

We came straight home and I made dinner, after dinner we went bowling. What a great day we had a blast.

The next day we slept in late, had breakfast then we played chess. A few hours later we headed over to Joeys house for Tony's party. I rang the doorbell Joey and his wife Angie greeted us. Then she brought Peter over to her grandchildren to play.

Joey's house was packed, people all around waiters were coming by with o'dourves and champagne you can hear the band playing on the outdoor porch from the living room. What a party!

Joey was introducing me to his family and friends. He joked around telling them I was his second son as he spoke in English. Then he spoke in Italian. I don't know exactly what he had said but the people's eyes kept on staring at me as they smiled and nodded their heads.

I walked over to Tony started to talk to him all of a sudden in the middle of our conversion Tony's wife Constance came over and started laughing and joking with Tony. Constance was asking Tony, when he was planning to return the baby boys clothes, he bought of his favorite baseball team. Then she said I don't think our beautiful daughter Tina would enjoy wearing them. We all could not stop laughing.

As I turned around I saw Duke and the Judge were talking to Pam Hayes. I walked over and started to smile.

Hey Tim.

Hey guys it's good to see you. It's been a while.

Same here Tim, then Pam hugged me so tight.

Tim your looking good how's it going?

Good Nancy.

I'm so glad you're here, it's nice to see you. Duke told me you been so busy at work.

Yes he is right there's been a lot of crazy case lately. The crime in our state Mississippi is getting worse, the economy is bad.

Tim I got to tell you. Duke and the guys talk about you all the time in a good way. The guys really missed you.

That's nice to hear thanks.

I really miss them so bad. I'm hoping that after I'm acquitted I will be back to visit everyone.

Tim I know what you're going through it is hard. Something will change soon you have a great defense team. Duke's been working hard trying to get more evidence.

You're right Nancy, thanks.

Duke was still talking to Pam when Joey walked over to us excused me, Duke I need to see you in my office for a few minutes. Can you break away?

Sure Joey.

I need your help! There is a new trash company trying to run me out of town and trying to steal my customer.

Sure let's go.

Is everyone having a nice time?

Yes Joey.

Pam is there anything else I can get you? Then they both started to laugh.

I got what I wanted then she clutched on to my arms, thanks to you Joey. Then everyone was laughing as Pam gave a blink of the eye to Joey.

Don't forget everyone the o'dourves are in the other room. Dinner will be in a little while.

Hey Dad, is it ok if I go downstairs in the basement with my new friends? We are going to play with their new T box game that everyone at school is talking about.

Sure Peter, before you go I want you to meet my friends. This is my son Peter. Then Peter went around shaking hands with everyone. Then when Peter came up to Pam he said are you my Dads new girlfriend?

Yes I am.

I need to tell you a secret, Peter went over to Pam and whispered something in her ear when he was through he turned around and then saw Duke at the other side of the room.

He yelled out to Uncle Duke, wait for me talk to you, then he ran over to him.

Peter how are you doing?

You are getting so tall young man. Peter are you adjusting to your new home?

Yes, but I wish I could live with my Dad.

Maybe one of these days you will. Uncle Duke, I need to talk to you.

Then Joey said Peter do you want me to leave, so you can talk to Uncle Duke.

No Joey you can stay.

What's up Peter?

Uncle Duke my Dad did not kill anyone! As Peter voice got louder people stop talking, they just stood there in a circle munching on the food listening to Peter. The kids at my school are saying to me my Dad is a killer and he is going to prison. Uncle Duke please help my Dad win his case, then Peter started crying as he hugged Duke

Peter we all know that your Dad is not a killer he is a great Dad. I'm working hard on your Dad's case to prove that he didn't kill anyone, but it's going to take me sometime. Peter, everything is going to work out trust me.

Thank you uncle Duke. He wiped the running tears off his face with his sleeves.

Then Tony's kids came up to Peter, and said we have been looking for you Peter, are you coming with us to play. Yes I will follow you guys.

Pam and I and Judge Nancy walked over closer early where Peter and Joey and Duke were talking.

We were standing behind some people, Peter could not see us. We were able to here every word Peter told Duke. Then Judge Nancy started to open her pocket book grabbed some tissue and handed a piece to Pam as they both wipe the tears from their faces.

Then Judge Nancy walked over to Duke and started crying as she hugged Duke then he started to comfort her. I could tell that he Judge was thinking about her young son Sam that had passed away years ago.

Duke called Tiny to come over.

Tiny excused himself as he was rapping and joking with Amy from Joey's office they seemed to hit it off.

Excused me Joe just for a minute before we go into your office I need to talk to Tiny?

Sure no problem Duke,

Tiny I need for you to go to Peter school tomorrow morning. Have a talk with the principal about who are these kids harassing Peter about Tim. Then Duke explained what was going on. This crap needs to stop now.

Yes sir you got it. I will take care of this problem boss.

I know you well.

Thank you.

10-4 Boss.

Oh Tiny, one more thing I need to tell you.

What's that Boss?

Don't mess with Joey's help. Then Duke started laughing so loud as they all started to laugh.

Then Joey told Tiny it was ok to see Amy. That Duke was busting his balls.

Don't listen to Duke, Amy is a sweet cute young lady, with a great sense of humor she is one of my best workers.

Pam and I started to walk over to the o'dourves table when we ran into Victor and Tammy.

Hey Tim.

Hey guys then I introduced Pam to Victor and Tammy.

Then Pam asked Tammy how was her fight? It was good but I got my ass kicked as you can see my black eye. But I also kicked her ass with a knock out in the fourth round. Congratulations!

Thanks.

Tammy you need to keep your baby face blocked the entire time sweetheart.

I know Victor but for my first fight I did well.

Yea, babe you're right. That maybe your last fight anyway so your old man will be nicer to us. Then he laughed.

Very funny Victor.

Oh Tim thanks for doing the route yesterday for us.

Sure anytime.

Well my Mon and Dad is supposed to come to the party but I think they went back home to New Haven.

I know, Joey and Angie are expecting them to be here.

Mom told me she had talked to Angie, last night they were coming.

What happen?

Victor and I went out to breakfast this morning with Mom and Dad.

Dad is pissed at me when he saw my black and blue eye. I told both of them that I was boxing Dad kind of went off on Victor.

What do you mean kind of? Your father did!

This is the first time I had ever let anyone chewed me out without me hitting them? What we do for love. Ha! ha.!

Chapter Twenty One

Not Again

It was Monday April 2nd 2014 8:00 am. I was sitting in the courtroom before the crowd came in. Trying to get my thoughts together I could not help but to keep on thinking what I would do if I'm convicted. These horrible thoughts are going through my mind that kept on haunting me. My court case has been dragging out for a few more months. Between people getting sick and the Judge is burning up his personal time and sick time before he retires. There are only four witnesses left. I'm still looking guilty. I was staring up at the ceiling and I started praying asking the man upstairs for his help.

Good morning Tim.

Good morning Ron.

Tim how was Tony's party yesterday?

We had a great time, it was fun.

Before I could say anything more the courtroom was getting crowded and loud.

Bam! Bam! Quiet in this courtroom the Judge yelled.

Please take your seats and let's get started.

Then, Judge Bailey was looking straight ahead as he pointed his gavel at me yelling out in his loud nasty voice we are not in a party, we are in a courtroom!

Let's get started.

Counselors please approach the bench!

Good morning gentlemen.

Good morning Judge.

Is there anything new going on with this case that I should be aware of gentlemen?

No your Honor.

All set your Honor.

Okay Counselors, Thank you.

Counselor Jackson you may call your witness.

Thank you your Honor.

Sergeant Dick Martian to the stand please.

Good morning, Sergeant Martian.

Good Morning,Counselor Jackson.

Could you tell the court how you are involved in Mr. Hall case?

I was called out to the crime scene on January 6, 2014 at 11:15 pm for Mr. Hall dead body. I collected the entire DNA from Mr. Hall's before his body was moved.

What did you found Sgt?

The accused Mr. Ripple finger prints was all over Mr. Hall's dead body.

Was there any other DNA found on Mr. Hall body?

Yes Counselor, dry up body fluid from a woman named Mrs Shea

Tell the court about Mrs.Shea .

She was brought in for questioning on January 8 th, 2014 and what was the result of her investigation? Mr. Hall and Mrs. Shea were both at By Sea Motel on Ocean Drive on January 6th 2014. They both had checked in at 10 am. Mr. Hall left the motel at 4:00 pm Mrs. Shea had left the motel at 7:00 am the next morning. She caught a cab to the airport, jumped onto a plane, headed for Ohio to spend time with her daughter. Her story was checked out, she is not a suspect she was let go.

Thank you Sergeant Martian I have no more questions at this time.

Counselor, James, you may proceed.

Thank you. Your Honor.

Good morning Sgt. Martian. Let's back up could you please tell the court where did you find Mr. Hall dead body? Yes, in an alleyway two stores down from the café.

You do know Sergeant Martian that my client Tim Ripple and Joe Hall were fighting in the alleyway next to the café and the cleaners not two alleys down from the café.

Sergeant Martian was there any more DNA finger prints that you came across beside the two that you had mention?

Yes Counselor James there were two other partial finger prints that were not Mrs. Shea. We cannot use the prints since they're not full prints, there's no way to find out who they're from.

Sgt. Martian was there any witnesses that may have seen the killing of Mr. Hall that you're aware of?

Well sir there were one witness that said she saw two people running around the same time frame of the killing. One person ran south and the other person ran north.

Did this witness see any of their faces?

Like I put in my report Counselor James the witness was leaving the night club when she was walking on the street then this person that was running away had bumped into her and knocked her down.

Sgt. Martian you're not answering my question. It's not that hard of a question to answer!

Objection your Honor.

Counselor James is harassing my witness.

No I'm not your Honor.

Overruled Counselor Jackson.

Proceed, Counselor James.

Thank you, your Honor .

Sergeant Martian I have an innocent client here accused of murder and now we are finding out not only was Mr. Hall found dead in a different alleyway? Now you're telling the court there were two people seen running away from the crime scene, when my client was at the hospital getting his leg attended to?

Sergeant Martian is holding back information, Your Honor.

Sustain!

Sergeant Martian please answer the questions Counselor James is asking you and stop beating around the bush!

Yes your Honor.

According to the witness she said the person that went running the other way looked like a young man. By the way Sergeant Martin does this witness has a name?

It was very obvious that Ron is starting to get pissed off at Sergeant Martian.

Ron's voice is getting louder and louder as he walked over to the stand, looking at each of the jurors as he was able to get all of their attention.

Then he was yelling out questions to the Sargent from the other side of the courtroom.

Sergeant Martian had a pissed off look on his face, along with a sarcastic voice when he answered Ron's question.

Yes,I'm sorry Counselor James her name is Mary Fox.

So Mary saw Mr., Ripple?

Yes, the other person that was running away, bumped into Mary as she left the bar.

Mary claims it was the accuser Tim Ripple wearing a black hoodie

Sergeant Martian did you check out your witness clothes for DNA from the person that bumped into her?

Yes Counselor James I did! No luck the person had gloves on. It was freezing out that night.

Your Honor I ask for permission from court to subpoena this witness Mary Fox?

I would like to question her. I think there is more to this story than Sergeant Martian is saying.

Your Honor there goes Counselor James with his rude comments again.

I'm, sorry your Honor will the court please disregard my last statement from the record thank you.

Sergeant Martian please give Counselor James a copy of Mary Fox file.

Do you have any question Sergeant Martian?

No your Honor, I don't.

I could feel that I was about to sneeze. I tried to hold it back but no luck. I sneeze so hard and loud that Judge Baily looked at me and pointed his gavel once again at me.

I quickly tried to cover my nose with my hand and turned my face to the left it was too late the blood from my nose was dripping fast on to my tie.

Excuse me Mr. Ripple your nose is bleeding again.

Yes your Honor I'm sorry.

I'm going to adjourn this court session until next Thursday morning at 8:30 am then we will continue your case.

Mr. Ripple you have one week to go to the doctor to find out what the hell is wrong with your nose, and how this problem can be fixed.I want a copy of the doctor's report first thing Thursday morning.

Do I make myself clear?

Yes your Honor.

Mr. Ripple I don't want to hear any excuses either.

Bam! Bam! Court is dismissed. We will continue this case Thursday at 8:30 am.

As I was leaving the courtroom I called Joey told him what was going on. I had asked him if he called the medical center and within a few minute Joey had called me back and told me they're waiting for me.

CHAPTER TWENTY TWO

TIME IS RUNNING OUT

I t's Thursday morning and I'm running late, its 9:00 am and my alarm did not go off for 6:00am. I should have been in court at 8:30 am.

I didn't have time to take a shower I washed my face got dress fast and spray my clothes down with some great smelling cologne. I don't even have time to make my coffee.

Dam it, I need my coffee to function but decided to skip it. I ran to my truck jumped in and put the pedal to the metal speeding through the streets heading to the courthouse. I just drove through my third red traffic light. I only have two more blocks to go; I will finally be at the courthouse.

All of a sudden I heard a loud siren that scared the crap out of me. I looked in the rear view mirror; I saw flashing red lights on the cop was right behind me. It was impossible for me to pull over, there is only one lane on the road and parked cars on both side. Then I heard the cop yelling in his microphone for me to pull over now. Quickly

I turned into the hospital parking lot as he had followed me and called in my license plate in as he walked over.

I need to see your driver license and your insurance card. Then the officer put his left hand resting on his gun with the holster unlocked.

Do you know why I stop you son?

I think I do officer.

You ran through two red traffic lights on purpose. You're also speeding 60 mph when the speed limit was posted at 35 then to top it all off you blew through the school zone with flashing lights that were on in a 20 mph zone.

Officer please I can explain!

I'm on trial and running late for my court case. I was just trying to get there faster Judge Baily is a tough Judge.

Yes son I know all about Judge Baily?

But I'm sorry son that does not give you the right to do what you have done. You could cause a serious accident and someone one could have been killed? Here you are as he handed me a ticket.

Wow that a lot of money.

Son it could be worse. I could arrest you now and lock you up so stop your complaining. You can fight this ticket in court sign the back of it and mail it in. Then they will mail you back a court day. Good luck.

As the cop left I continue going down Washington Street. I quickly pulled into the court parking garage, took the parking ticket and parked my truck.

I ran quickly for the elevator headed for the third floor. I continue running through the hallway when I heard a guard yelling out to me stop you're running now. I grabbed the courtroom door and walked in fast all out of breath.

Excuse me Counselor James! Take your seat now please.

Yes your Honor.

Bam! Bam!

Well, Well Well, look who is finally here.

Your Honor, I can explain.

By all means the floor is yours Mr. Ripple and it better be good!

Thank you your Honor.

My alarm clock didn't go off I got up late. I quickly washed and got dress. As I was driving I was trying to find my phone so I could call Counselor James but realize that I had left it at the house. Then on top of all I was stopped by the police. Sorry I'm late your Honor.

Mr. Ripple what was the ticket for and how much was the fine?

Speeding and running through two red lights the fine is three hundred and twenty dollars!

Dam Mr. Ripple you're having a bad morning.

Yes, your Honor I am.

Do you have a copy of your doctor report for me? Or did you also forget it at home?

Yes I do have the report for you your Honor.

You may approach the bench I also want your ticket that you received this morning. Thank you young man, you may take your seat and let's continue.

Counselor, James.

Yes your Honor, Thank you.

Doctor Jones could you please point out to the court, the man you had treated at the hospital that night on January 6th, 2014

The gentleman that just walked in late that is Mr. Tim Ripple.

Thank you Doc.

So, Mr. Ripple came to the hospital that night?

Yes Sir.

What time was Tim with you Doctor? About 11:15 pm I cleaned his wound and ended up putting twenty stiches in his leg.

I had also cleaned the big laceration under his left eye, and put five stiches plus a patch over his eye.

So what time did he leave the hospital about 12:10 AM Thank you Doctor. I have no further questions at this time!

Counselor Jackson you may cross exam.

Thank you, your Honor.

Doctor did you asked Tim what happen to him?

Yes he told me he had a fight with the man who had killed his mother.

Doctor Jones after listening to Tim Ripple story after he left the hospital did you called the police and reported the incident?

No Counselor Jackson I did not.

Doctor Jones why not? If Mr. Ripple is wounded that bad, did it ever occurred to you how the other person he fought with is.

No Counselor Jackson. I'm a Doctor not a policeman!

Doctor Jones you said Mr. Ripple left the hospital at 12:10AM.

Yes Counselor.

Doctor Jones could you have mistaken the times that night because of the brownout in the hospital due to a lighting hitting a transformer early that night remember?

Objection your Honor Counselor Jackson is tormenting my client along with his sarcasm remarks.

Sustain.

You're right Counselor James.

Betty, please strike that last question Counselor Jackson just made from the court records.

Yes your Honor.

Thank you, Betty.

May I please speak your Honor?

Yes Doctor Jones go ahead.

I do know the time Mr. Ripple left. The young man had used my cell phone to call a taxi. Then he went into waiting room. When the taxi came he walked over to the cafeteria where I was having dinner. He thanked me then left. Mr. Ripple walked away as I took a call from my wife.

Thank you Doctor. I have no further question at this time. Doctor Jones you my take your seat now.

You may call your next witness Counselor James. Thank you your Honor.

Mary Fox to the stand please.

Good morning Miss Fox.

Good morning Sir.

Thank you for coming. Could you please tell the court is there someone here that bumped into you as you were leaving the café on January 6,2014

Could you please point to that person? Yes, the gentleman is in the right front row coughing his brains out now.

He is the man that bumped into me.

Miss Fox, what time did that happen?

Around 11:05pm.

What do you mean around Miss Fox? It seem like you're not so sure of the time this happen.

No I know it was 11:05pm.

And how is that Miss Fox?

When Mr. Ripple bumped in to me I was pushed to the ground hit my watch against the asphalt and it broke at11:05pm.

To this day my watch is still not working would you like to see it I have it here in my pocketbook? It's in my statement that the police have.

Counselor James you must not read my statement that I gave the police.

Yes Miss Fox I did read your statement. I'm just double checking with you. Miss Fox how many drink did you have that night before you left the café?

I drank three Long Island Ice Tea.

Wow that's a lot of liquor to assume in a short amount of time. According to public records, Miss Fox you were in rehab for alcohol for three-months you just go out. And this is your second time you were there. Am I reading your record's right Miss Fox?

Yes Counselor James

Two weeks later you're at the café drinking.

Objection your Honor my wittiness is not on trial it seem like Counselor James is forgetting this!

There is a discrepancy here your Honor, and I'm trying to find it.

Overrule!

Continue Counselor James.

Miss Fox did you hear Doctor Jones? He just testified that the man that you say that had bumped into you Tim Ripple was in the hospital with him between 10:30pm -12:05 am that night.

Miss Fox, can you please tell the court how can Mr. Ripple be at two places at the same time?

Objection, your Honor.

Counselor James is harassing my witness.

No I am not your Honor.

Overrule.

But your Honor?

Counselor Jackson, I said overruled.

Continue Counselor James.

Counselor James has a good point, continue.

Thank you your Honor.

Ron voice was getting louder and louder as he was walking backwards talking and is facing the jurors.

I'm sure, I'm not the only one here in this courtroom wants to know how this could be one person in two different places at the same time. For sure Ron had the entire juror's attention now. They all looked puzzled and confused as they watched Ron with his hand gesture while listening to his question I have no further question at this time thank you Miss Fox.

Counselor Jackson you may cross exam your witness now.

Thank you your Honor.

Miss Fox, have you ever seen Mr. Ripple before this incident had occurred?

No I haven't Counselor Jackson.

You know Miss Fox Tim Ripple did play the night before with a band at the café.

Maybe you saw him that night?

No Counselor Jackson I did not go to see that band that night I was out of town.

I swear I never saw Mr. Ripple until that night he bumped into me. I know Mr. Ripple bumped into me that night and I can prove it.

Your Honor may I have the court permission for my witness to prove her point.

Miss Fox you are under oath. Your fact better be accurate.

Yes your Honor.

Yes Counselor Jackson you have the court permission.

It better be good and if your information is incorrect I will dismiss this case and Mr. Ripple is free from all charges. So Counselor Jackson would you like to talk to Miss Fox before she makes her statement?

Yes your Honor I would thank you. Counselor Jackson walked over to Miss Fox as they both whispered to each other. The people in the courtroom were in shocked and puzzled waiting for Counselor Jackson answer. Your Honor

Yes Counselor Jackson.

Miss Fox will prove her facts now.

Okay Counselor Jackson lets continue.

Go ahead Miss Fox the floor is yours.

I saw that night when Mr. Ripple knocked me down as I turned my head I notice a big birth mark shape like a heart on the left side bottom of his neck. He was wearing a tank top

Your Honor I ask you permission for Tim Ripple to stand up and undo his tie and unbutton his shirt and let the court see this birth mark on the left side of his neck.

Permission is granted Counselor Jackson.

Objection your Honor that's irritates my client. This is unheard of taking his shirt off.

Overrule Counselor James!

Mr. Ripple please show the court your neck. If you have to take your tie off and unbutton your shirt, do so please.

Do you have any question Mr. Ripple?

No, your Honor.

I started taking off my tie the whole court room was quite watching me as if I was a stripper at a club. I felt embarrassed. I unbutton my dress shirt when I heard the juror and some of the people in courtroom made a loud noise when they saw my heart shape birth mark on my neck.

Thank you, Mr. Ripple you may button up your shirt and have your seat.

Yes your Honor.

Objection your Honor. This is freaking crazy.

Watch you language Counselor James!

My client was at the hospital. We all heard the doctor testimony.

Your Honor.

Yes Counselor Jackson, you may speak.

Then how can my witness describe Mr. Ripple birthmark to a tee?

Maybe someone told Miss Fox they were there when Mr. Ripple was fighting with Mr. Hall when he took off his shirt as he got into the cab heading for the hospital.

No Your Honor, my client Tim Ripple had his shirt and jacket on that night of the fight the video shows that. He is being set up your Honor. It was pitch black that night at 11:05pm there were no street light in front of the café. The street light pole in front of the café was hit and knocked over by a drunk driver two nights before the killing. It took the city three weeks later to put a new light pole up. Your Honor there is no way Miss Fox saw my client birth mark.

Counselor Jackson please wait until Counselor James is through talking before you start talking.

Yes your Honor.

Anyone could have told Miss Fox about his birth mark. Your Honor Miss Fox could have seen my client Mr. Ripple on the internet with the band on one of those social blogs.

I have no further questions thank you Miss Fox.

You may take your seat Miss Fox.

Thank you Counselor Jackson.

As I turned to my right side Duke was waving to me as he bend over whispering to Ron then handed him some papers.

Bam! Bam!

Counselor James what seem to be the problem over there?

Well your Honor we just received some good news from the FBI. They were able to find the third DNA. They had picked up the killer two days ago we have here a full written confession from him. His name is Mr. Shea he went after Mr. Hall for two reasons. Mr. Hall was having an affair with Mr Sheas's wife. And the other reason was Mr. Hall owed Mr.Shea one hundred thousand dollars on a gamble debt, he never paid up. The police picked Mr. Shea up in Florida.

Your Honor could you please release my client Tim Ripple from his charges and have his record clean as soon as possible? My client will be taking the bar exam in a few month. Councilor James approach the bench please I need to read that paper work before I can release Mr. Ripple.

Yes your Honor.

Bam! Bam! Quite in this courtroom now!

Betty please let it be known for the court records in today case number 70231 that Mr. Tim Ripple is innocent and is free from all charges. And drop all charges from his record. I will make a copy of Mr. Shea's confession and put it in the file with Mr. Ripple release paper, is there any question from anyone?

Your Honor what time can we get a copy of the release papers?

Well Counselor James the court case papers will not be ready to release until three weeks from today. They will be up on the third floor in the records department.

Thank you your Honor.

Does anyone else has any question please speak now I'm all ears?

Your Honor.

Yes Miss Juror number four please stand up how can I help you?

Well your Honor I'm happy Mr. Ripple is free. I'm still puzzled by Miss Fox fact. How did she know Mr. Ripple had that heart birth mark?

Miss that is a good question, but it is not relevant to the case anymore it's over now.

Thank you your Honor.

Is there any more questions from anyone? Go ahead young lady with your hand up please stand.

Your Honor may I please have my phone back?

No Miss your phone is already gone to charity. You may take your seat thank you.

I would like to thank everyone for your time for being here. Mr. Ripple I would like to see you in my chamber?

Yes your Honor.

Bam! Bam! Court is now adjourned.

Congratulation Tim thanks Ron.

Hey Tim, Joey told all us we will meet at Mama Mia's restaurant he reserved the backroom for us.

Ok Duke,I will see you guys there.

I have to go now and see what the Judge wants. as I Knocked he yelled come in Tim have a seat I will be right with you he was finishing going through his email on his smart phone. I just sat there wondering what the hell the Judge has to say to me now.

Tim how you doing son?

A lot better now your Honor.

Tim I'm going to get your ticket squashed, you won't have to pay the fine and you will not receive any points on your license. This ticket also will kept you from taking your bar exam.

Thank you, Judge Baily for taking care of it for me.

We shook hands I open the door ready to walk out when two cops were standing in the doorway asking me if Judge Baily here? As he was right behind me answering, yes how can I help you gentlemen?

As they walked into his office I walk out into the hallway shutting the door. I stop quickly and bend down and pretending to tie my shoes. I listened through the close door. I heard one of cops was telling the Judge about his grandson Mark Heal had overdosed on heroin last night and was found dead. Next I heard loud noise like the Judge pounding his hands on something maybe his desk then he started to yell and cry.

I then left and headed for the restaurant to meet everyone. I was so happy. I call Peter to let him know the great news

Life was getting better. It still had it's up and down but the ups were more on my side. I went at the restaurant eat and drank and had a great time with all my friends.

I had passed the Connecticut bar exam six months later. Ron and I became partners we open up our practice down from Joey's Company. Joey fired attorney Jackson and hired us. He is our best client.

Joey's case is big. Ron and I represent him of his invention burning trash and turning it into electricity. The local electricity company finally bought the plant from Joey. Boy, did we receive a nice check.

Duke also asked me if we could represent his club in Detroit. Judge Nancy Johnson is so nice she helped me to study for my bar exam and sent me a copy of the state laws. So I could study and pass the Michigan bar exam.

Eight months later I flew down to Michigan passed the bar exam. Duke gave me free rent he had an empty apartment I made it our new law office. I hired a few lawyers to run the office so I can come and go back and forth to Connecticut.

My son Peter was doing good. I have full custody of him because my ex-wife was abusing him.

Life is full of surprises.

One day I was in my office when Mr. Dell from Surf and Turf restaurant walked in. He apologized to me for the way he was yelling at me in his restaurant that night I was arrested. He handed me an envelope with five thousand cash as a retainer to represent him whenever he needs my services. He told me people today are always looking to sue and he is worried about his restaurant.

I received a call from Tony's attorney, Pat Cole he was the one I hired to handle my case with the printing company. He had won my case. He sued the printing company that put my information on the milk cartons. Attorney Cole did a great job.

It's my company now, and I was going to keep my word. I was in the process of putting up the billboards on highway 91 north and south thanking the owner for his printing company that I own now.

Pam left her city job in Mississippi, moved here in Connecticut and is now working at Joey's trash company.

My twin sister Sue also moved into town. We both spend a lot of time together catching up for the times we lost not growing up together. We were on a roll to find a brother we were told we have.

Ron and I had hired Sue as the office manager it is working out great. Pam and I are engaged along with Duke and Judge Nancy, we are planning a double wedding.

Duke had asked Tiny to stay in Connecticut and open up a new chapter for the club. Duke bought a building in Hartford off South Street where Tiny built a beautiful club house.

Tiny was also on Joey's payroll, what he was doing I never asked I didn't want to know.

LIFE IS GOOD.

CPSIA information can be obtained at www.ICGtesting.com
Printed in the USA
BVOW05s2356010416

442684BV00008B/70/P

9 781495 805202